Beyond the Rainbow Flash

Book 1 in the Flash Travelers Series

Andrew Connan

Published by Dogs Breath Press, LLC
www.AndrewConnan.com

Beyond the Rainbow Flash
Book 1 in the *Flash Travelers Series*

ISBN: 978-0-9968362-6-5

This is a work of fiction.

See also: www.AndrewConnan.com

Contents

Prologue: Terrified Sailors

The crew of the square-rigged ship looked over their shoulders in terror and frantically hauled on the lines to wring every bit of speed out of their vessel. The wooden hull and masts of the ship groaned under the strain, and the sails nearly burst as she shot forward. When the ship had gained as much speed as the captain thought she could stand, he swung the wheel hard. The ship heeled over, raising the guns to bear on their foe. The guns boomed, and cannon balls flew directly at their target, but the target moved deftly, and they did no damage.

As soon as their foe landed on the ship's deck, the wind went out of the ship's sails, and she stopped dead. He reached inside his jacket, took out a pen, and carried out his terrible revenge.

Two hundred years later...

Chapter 1. A Fearful Boy

Sam slouched on the cool, smooth wooden bench in his elementary school's playground, pen in hand and his battered spiral notebook in his lap, trying to write a poem to go with a story. Sam wrote wonderful stories, or at least he thought he did, but he never showed them to anyone except his parents, fearing that the other kids would think they were stupid and laugh at him. He daydreamed too much to make sense of math or science, or to compete in sports or games, so he spent a lot of time sitting alone thinking up stories.

While his classmates romped in the sunny playground, Sam worked on a poem to go with a tale about a new, courageous character he had recently thought up named Danger Dog:

> Danger Dog flew through the thunder and
> lightning
> While his flashlight steadily lost all its
> brightening.

No, no, that's awful, he thought. He crossed it out and tried again:

> Danger Dog flew through the thunder and
> lightning,
> Even though his undies were steadily tight-
> ening.

Much worse! He crossed it out and tried once more:

> Danger Dog flew through the thunder and
> lightning.
> He knew he must win though the journey
> was frightening.

Yes! Much better, he told himself.

Sam yearned for a dog, but his mother refused, so he dreamed up a loyal, trustworthy, and brave dog of his own. Sam thought of himself as loyal and trustworthy, but he knew he had trouble being brave. Though he dreamed of being fearless, or at least brave enough to do what the other kids did, his imagination kept getting in the way.

Through Sam's eyes, all the boys who played kick-ball towered nine feet above him and kicked the ball so hard they bashed holes in the school's concrete walls. Sam imagined that his teacher soared fifteen feet above him so terrifyingly that even Sam's pencils ran away. To Sam the principal resembled a toupee-wearing *Tyrannosaurus rex,* who lumbered down the hall with feet so big he could crush a kid like a bug.

Sam persuaded himself that the slide in the playground would accelerate him to the speed of light and blast him through the space-time dimensional rift (whatever that was). He imagined the chains on the swings would turn into anacondas, wrap themselves around his neck, and choke him to death. Such things never happened to the other kids, and Sam himself played on the slide and swings. But he couldn't stop picturing those horrible things happening to him. Because of his fears, Sam stayed in the shadows and dreamed up stories.

Even after school, when all the other kids saw a bus pull up to the curb, Sam saw a giant yellow kid eater, with the door as its mouth. He watched in horror as his classmates climbed heedlessly into the beast's diesel-scented maw, but he forced himself to board the bus anyway so he could get home.

Late that warm autumn afternoon, Sam lay on his stomach on the boulder in his back yard. A small section of the giant white and tan rock, about 40 feet long and about five feet high, rose above the surrounding lawn. Sam's dad told him that the bolder was a left-over from the last ice age, but Sam didn't care. He just liked being on it and imagining that it was a rocket ship to far off places.

He rested his chin on his hands and gazed at tiny green insects fluttering through the air, their gossamer wings glowing in the last thin rays of autumn daylight.

He tried to think of a good villain for his Danger Dog story. Sam believed that evil people were easy to spot. After all, in comics and cartoons they looked so obviously wicked. Sam thought about making Danger Dog's enemy similar to the vile characters in the comics. He would make his bad guy Bug Man, a huge, six-legged monster with shiny green armor, enormous muscles, a window-shattering voice, and glowing yellow bug eyes.

As Sam lay there absorbed in thought, his dad, a tall, rumpled man with a ready smile and big, gentle hands came home from work. He ambled over and said, "Hey Sam, I've got a surprise for you. Let's get in the car."

As they strolled to the car, Sam's dad said, "You've worked hard these past few months and did your chores every day without being asked. So, I've finally convinced your mother that you are responsible enough to get a puppy from the pound."

"Yes!" Sam shouted with glee. He danced around the lawn, and sang a song he had made up hoping this day would come:

A dog! A dog! I'm gonna get a dog!
I might just go and name him Spot.
I'll pick up poop that stinks a lot.

We'll swim together when it's hot.
We'll play all day until we drop.
We'll take long naps upon my cot.
A dog, a dog, a dog!

Sam's dad laughed and applauded.

"I'll take really good care of him," Sam added. "Can I get any dog I want?"

"Yes, but remember, we want a healthy one. We can't afford big vet bills."

"Are we going now?"

"Yep."

"Yahoo!"

As they walked to the car Sam's dad gave him a little tickle under the chin. Sam giggled and hugged his dad.

Chapter 2. Fascinating New Friends

Sam and his dad stood in the animal shelter's empty reception room until a lady dressed in a sweatshirt, jeans, and sneakers marched briskly in through a side door. Her short brown hair, nice smile, and twinkling eyes reminded Sam of his grandmother. He liked her immediately. She carried a clipboard and said, "I'll be with you as soon as I finish supervising the unloading of this shipment of puppy food."

On the wall, Sam noticed a large bulletin board with snapshots of happy people and their grinning dogs. Studying the pictures, he tried to imagine what it would be like having his very own dog. He imagined playing outside with the dog, but his musings were cut short by a jab of dread. What if his new dog found out that almost everything scared him? Immediately he laughed at himself. He thought, *That's silly. It's just a dog. What does a dog know, right?*

When the lady came back to the reception room, she asked, "Now, how can I help you?"

"I'm Steven Foster, and this young man is my son Sam. He would like to adopt a puppy," said Sam's dad.

"That's great! I'm very pleased to meet you, Sam. My name is Ms. Wright, and I'm the manager of this shelter."

They shook hands.

"What kind of dog did you have in mind?"

Sam shrugged. "I don't know."

"Well, I'm certain we can find just the right puppy for you."

They entered a big room that smelled of dog and echoed with yips and barks. Ms. Wright left them there to look around and she headed back to the front desk.

Sam's dad instructed, "Now you and I will search for a nice, healthy puppy."

Sam thought for a moment, made up a little poem, and said to his dad:

> "I want to look around alone, to see which
> dog I'd like to own."

Mr. Foster laughed and said. "That's pretty good. OK, Sam, this can be your choice, but remember, healthy."

He went to a corner to flip through old issues of *Dog* magazine.

Sam wandered around and eventually wound up in the very back of the room. A sign hanging over an open doorway read: Do Not Enter - Authorized Personnel Only. Even though this message looked very official and sounded scary, it also made Sam curious. He peered inside what looked like a small, dimly lit cave with drab gray walls and a worn linoleum floor. The cramped chamber smelled of coffee and had a sign that read Keep This Break Room Clean. The room held several cages lined up on the floor, a wall-mounted television tuned to a news channel, a table and chairs, a coffee machine, and a little refrigerator.

Suddenly a voice called out, “Hey, kid. Over here.”

“Who’s there?” Sam asked, his whole body alert to danger. He hunched his shoulders and pulled his jacket tightly around him.

“Come to the middle cage, kid,” the voice continued.

Although Danger Dog could speak, Sam had never envisioned a real dog talking to him. As curious as he was scared, he inched into the room despite the intimidating sign. As he approached the middle cage, he saw an enormous dog with a long, narrow snout, big, pointy ears, a thick gray and tan coat, and a long, bushy tail. The moment Sam saw him he thought he looked a lot like a huge coyote.

In his cage sat a very nice-looking teddy bear with a thick middle which, Sam thought, made the teddy bear appear powerful rather than fat. Sam couldn’t shake the impression that the teddy bear looked at him with great intelligence.

"You talk!" Sam finally exclaimed, stepping cautiously to the cage.

"Yes, we can."

"We?"

"Yes. My name is Randolph Coyote the Third, and this is my friend, Bobbie Bear."

The teddy bear waved and said, "Hello."

Despite his astonishment at hearing them both speak, Sam politely introduced himself, "Hi. My name is Sam."

"Pleased to meet you, Sam," Bobbie Bear responded, with a slight bow.

"Does everybody always call you Randolph Coyote the Third all the time?"

"Naw, Randolph is fine."

"How did you guys learn to talk?" Sam asked, glancing over his shoulder. He worried that his father might come looking for him and see him speaking with an animal.

Randolph shrugged and answered, "I don't know. We could always talk. How did *you* learn to talk?"

Sam shrugged and laughed.

Bobbie Bear said, "We would greatly appreciate it if you would select us and get us out of this cage Randolph got us into."

"Me!" exclaimed Randolph Coyote the Third. "I did not! How would I know that guy was a dogcatcher? Besides, he looked friendly to me."

Bobbie Bear snapped back, "Do you recall our original reason for being here? Remember that business at Muckjumper Bay?" Bobbie Bear turned to Sam and explained, "Randolph thought he possessed the loudest sneeze in all the worlds, so he got into a sneezing contest. He bet a fortune, which we didn't have. He bet that he could sneeze louder than an elephant!"

Randolph replied defensively, "He wasn't a very big elephant."

"But we fled from that elephant and his pals, as well as our friends and our jobs, and we can never go back to that port!"

"There are plenty of other ports. This is one we're at right now."

Bobbie Bear almost exploded and spat out, "This is not a port—this is nowhere! We came here because it is so remote no one else ever comes here! The Rainbow Flash is the dead end of the hinterlands, the outskirts of the back-waters, the most obscure—"

"Excuse me," Sam half whispered, certain that a grown-up would come marching into the room at any moment. "What's the Rainbow Flash?"

Randolph explained to Sam, "That's where you are. There are lots of known worlds, and the one you're in is called the Rainbow Flash. If you really want to find out more about it, get us out of this cage and take us home with you. We'll not only tell you what a flash is, we'll take you through one."

"We should not do that!" Bobbie Bear hissed under her breath.

"Don't listen to her," Randolph said to Sam. "It's no problem, really."

"So, what are you?" Sam asked Randolph.

"I'm part wolf and part coyote. I've kept the family name of Coyote but I call myself whatever works at the moment, wolf, coyote, or dog."

Sam said, "You're certainly not a coyote. I see plenty of coyotes when I visit my grandparents in New Mexico. You're much, much bigger than they are. You might pass for an enormous wolf, but you're way too big to be a coyote."

"Really? I'm average size where I come from. I gotta have a talk with your coyotes and find out why they're so puny."

Sam thought for a moment and reasoned, "If you two can talk, why don't you just ask the animal shelter people to let you go?"

Bobbie Bear answered, "Excellent question. We have been debating just that point. We are not certain how things work here. The fact that we were captured and are now in this cage is proof of that. If we speak and ask to be let go, we might find ourselves in worse trouble. After watching the news for three days, we know that scientists here do terrifying things to animals in laboratories. We're scared they might turn us over to one of those places. Besides, if the people here knew we could talk, they would quickly find out what a flash is and how to use them. We would be in terrible trouble with the Inter-flash Council. That is why we need you to get us out of here."

"Besides," Randolph Coyote the Third added solemnly, "I heard them say this afternoon that they plan to put me down tomorrow morning."

"What does 'put down' mean?" Sam asked.

Bobbie Bear explained, "It means kill."

Shocked and worried, Sam replied, "They plan to kill you in the morning? That's terrible!"

"What are you doing in here?"

Sam jumped with surprise and turned around to see Ms. Wright scowling down at him.

"The sign is quite clear. You are not allowed in this room."

Sam's mind raced to think up an excuse for being in the room, as Mr. Foster sauntered in with an amused expression.

Sam summoned all his courage in defense of Randolph Coyote the Third and exclaimed, "That dog can talk!"

Sam's dad said, "Now, Sam, we know you have an excellent imagination, but ..."

"No, no! I heard him! He told me his name is Randolph Coyote the Third and the bear's name is Bobbie Bear, and Bobbie Bear can walk and talk and everything! Come on, Randolph, talk!" Sam insisted.

Randolph sat stock still, totally confused. If he talked, the animal shelter might let them out, or maybe send them off to a lab to be dissected. Bobbie Bear knew for certain that they would be better off going home with Sam, so she sat motionlessly.

Ms. Wright took a deep breath and explained, "We aren't sure if this is a dog or a coyote or what. When our people picked him up, he refused to let go of the teddy bear. Rather than fight him we just let him keep the stuffed animal. At any rate, this room is strictly off limits. I suggest you find a puppy in the main room."

Sam felt crushed and confused. He believed in following rules, and Ms. Wright seemed angry with him, which terrified him. But he knew he must do something. He couldn't just let Randolph Coyote the Third die.

To further convince Sam, Randolph Coyote the Third let out an imploring, "Yip, yip?"

Without thinking, Sam declared, "I'll take him."

Sam's dad said, "There is no way we are having that, that, whatever it is in our house. That's the scariest looking animal I have ever seen. Just look at the size of him!"

"Dad, it's perfectly safe to be around him."

"How do you know that?"

"We spoke for a few minutes. He's quite civilized."

Sam's dad closed his eyes, rubbed his forehead, and shook his head slowly while groaning.

Ms. Wright tried hard not to laugh, but she couldn't help chuckling a little. She loved dogs and wanted to see them adopted rather than put down. Hoping to place this animal in a good home, she opened the cage door. Randolph trotted out and sat by her side.

She scratched him behind the ears and said, "He may strike you as big and tough, but he's really a sweetie pie. In the three days he's been here he has exhibited absolutely no aggressive or violent behavior. In fact, we've let him play with the other dogs, all of them much smaller. He's playful but very patient with them. We just can't keep him. If I didn't have five dogs of my own already, I'd adopt him. I have the feeling he's very special, but he's so big and wild looking people flee at the first sight of him. I very much want to find a home for him, and Sam is clearly comfortable around him. Besides, he does the funniest trick. Watch this."

Ms. Wright went to a box in the corner and took out a tennis ball. She put it on the floor in front of Randolph and commanded, "Bounce."

Randolph picked up the ball with his mouth, flipped it into the air, and bounced it repeatedly on the top of his snout. After the last bounce he snapped it high in the air, caught it with his mouth, and set it on the floor in its original place.

Sam and his dad laughed and applauded. Mr. Foster said, "That's spectacular, but my wife expects us to bring home a puppy."

"I understand that, but this big guy is a great dog and well trained. By the way, have you ever tried to house-break a puppy?"

Sam's dad shook his head no.

"It takes more time, patience, and cleanups than you can imagine. Along with all his other skills, I know this big guy is housebroken."

Sam went over to Randolph Coyote the Third, wrapped his arms around the animal's massive neck, and buried the side of his head in the thick fur. He looked at his dad, and begged, "Please? You said it could be my choice."

"No, I don't think so."

"Dad, you always taught me a deal's a deal."

Sam's dad sighed. "Are you sure, Sam?"

"Yes."

Mr. Foster thought for a long moment, shook his head and rolled his eyes, then said, "Fine. We'll take . . . what's his name?"

"Randolph Coyote the Third."

"That's quite a mouthful. How did you come up with that name?"

"I didn't. He told me his name."

Sam's dad understood Sam's imagination, so he

replied, "Right, of course. Well, anyway we'll take him and the stuffed animal."

"You mean Bobbie Bear."

"Sure. Him, too."

"Daaaad, Bobbie Bear is a girl."

Sam's dad decided not to disagree.

Ms. Wright beamed with pleasure.

Randolph gave Sam's face a huge, wet lick. Sam happily yelled, "Yech!" as he wiped his face with his hand.

When Sam reached into the cage to lift Bobbie Bear out he expected her to be like any other teddy bear, but she wasn't. Her heavy weight and hard body astonished him. He had to struggle for a moment to move her. That made him even more curious about his new friends.

After Sam's dad signed the papers he bought a collar and leash from the animal shelter. The four of them went out into the crisp, autumn air fragrant with the smell of leaves that crunched under their feet. Sam, carrying Bobbie Bear, watched Randolph wag his bushy tail and strut to show off his good looks. Sam's determination had saved Randolph Coyote the Third's life, a marvelous first for Sam. As he strolled next to his new dog, he felt like he had become as big and strong as Randolph.

Sam watched Bobbie Bear as she looked all around her at this alien landscape of parking lots, cars, and highways. To Sam she seemed to absorb everything all at once.

When they got home they entered through the

kitchen, Sam's mom's bastion of order and cleanliness. Recently scrubbed, the kitchen floor gleamed. Neatly arranged ingredients stood at attention in their assigned places, and a dozen cooking utensils hung neatly over the stove. The warm kitchen smelled of cookies baking. A small stack of reports waited on the table for Sam's mom to read before work at the hospital the next morning.

Sam's mom cut up lettuce with a large knife. Immediately she stopped cutting, took one look at Randolph Coyote the Third, and exclaimed, "What is *that?*"

Chapter 3. Hello & Goodbye

"He's my new dog . . ." Sam murmured.

Sam's mom stood with arms crossed, feet planted on the floor, and her knife held like a weapon. Sam couldn't tell which she disapproved of more, the enormous beast that sauntered into her kitchen or her husband for bringing him there. Scowling at Randolph Coyote the Third, she stated, "That is not a dog, that is a huge coyote or a wolf. That is a wild animal and does not belong in a house, let alone anywhere near a child."

Sam thought, *I don't know if Randolph is a dog or a coyote, but I do know he isn't a wild animal.*

"And what is that?" Sam's mom asked, pointing her knife at the teddy bear.

"Oh, this is Bobbie Bear. Bobbie Bear and Randolph Coyote the Third are friends and travel together," Sam explained.

"Well, at least the teddy bear is very nice looking," Sam's mom replied.

Though Bobbie Bear had planned to remain silent,

she replied, without thinking, "Thank you."

"Did you say that?" Sam's mom asked Sam.

"No, Bobbie Bear did."

Sam's mom replied, "Very funny."

Sam quickly tried to think of a way to convince his mother to let him keep his new friends. Randolph Coyote the Third and Bobbie Bear remained silent, and Sam realized they decided to keep their ability to speak a secret.

"Mom, do we have any tennis balls?"

"No, of course not. None of us plays tennis."

Sam thought for a moment, and then commanded, "Randolph Coyote the Third sit!"

He sat.

"Lie down."

He lay down.

"Roll over to your left."

He rolled over to his left.

"Roll over to your right."

He rolled over to his right.

"Jump up and go woof."

He jumped up and let out a happy, friendly woof. Then, without being asked, he took Bobbie Bear gently in his mouth, tossed her in the air, and caught her so that she straddled his snout. He flipped her in the air and caught her again on his snout, but this time she landed upside down, balancing on her right paw. He flipped her one more time, and she did a double back flip and landed perfectly, straddling Randolph's shoulders.

Sam and his dad laughed and applauded. Sam's mom smiled grudgingly.

"You have to admit, Joanie," said Mr. Foster, "That's quite a display."

"He certainly is well trained," she admitted. "He can stay for now, but he goes back at the first sign of trouble."

"Yippee!" cried Sam.

"Now go to your room and do your homework," said Sam's mom. "I'll call you when dinner is ready."

Sam ran off to his room with his two new friends.

Sam's room held a wilderness of half-finished, broken, and abandoned experiments and creative projects. Long ago, Sam's mom had given up trying to keep it tidy and made areas of it into no-clean zones.

The crammed floor contained:

The few remaining pieces of a chess set (Sam disliked chess since he spent most of each game daydreaming and always got clobbered).

Parts of model trains and track of different gauges from when he had wanted to write stories about railroading.

A wand and paper top hat from a magic set he thought would lead him into enchanted realms but turned out to be nothing more than trickery.

Stacks of paperback adventure stories from a used

bookstore, each of which he had consumed in a single sitting.

Piles of stories Sam himself had written, none of which he had shown to anyone at school.

Dozens of partially finished drawings of dogs, pigs, horses, and motor scooters, all of them flying.

A half-completed model pirate ship that Sam hadn't quite gotten around to assembling.

Pieces of a model airplane he had found in the park—the wings in one trashcan, the body in another.

Parts of an electric drill his dad had dropped from a ladder while trying to repair their leaky roof, sending the body in one direction and the motor in another.

The walls were covered with maps and blueprints Sam's dad had brought home from work.

Randolph Coyote the Third sniffed around the floor looking for a place to lie down but couldn't find one he liked. Finally, he hopped onto the bed, circled three times, scratched behind his ear with his hind paw, and stretched out on the covers, taking up almost the entire length of the bed. He yawned and looked around. "Nice place. Think you can cram any more stuff in here?"

Sam laughed and set Bobbie Bear on the bed next to his teddy bear. Bobbie Bear turned to the teddy bear and said, "Hello, my name is Bobbie Bear. I am very pleased to meet you."

The teddy bear did not respond.

She repeated, “Hello, my name is Bobbie Bear. What is your name?”

Again, no response.

Bobbie Bear turned to Sam and asked, “Is he alright?”

Sam smiled and explained, “Teddy bears here don’t talk or do any of the things you can do.”

“Really? Why not?”

“Teddy bears here have nothing inside them but pillow stuffing. Pick him up and give him a squeeze, and you’ll see what I mean.”

Bobbie Bear did and remarked, “What a peculiar world you live in.”

Sam giggled and said, “I’ll get some food for Randolph. Can I bring you anything?”

“Thank you for your kind offer, but I do not eat food. I have crystals inside me that give me all the energy I need,” Bobbie Bear explained.

Randolph added, “Bobbie has a couple of spare sets of crystals. When one set runs down, she replaces it with a charged set and leaves the weak crystals out in the sunshine until they’re recharged. It’s a pretty good system.”

After Sam returned from the kitchen and Randolph had eaten, Bobbie Bear said to Sam, “Well, we will depart now. Many thanks for your great assistance. We are in your debt.”

Chapter 4. Flight Training

"You're leaving? But you promised to take me through a flash," Sam said.

Randolph Coyote the Third whispered to Bobbie Bear, "The kid has a point, and this isn't such a bad setup. Sam and his parents seem OK, and we could use this time to look around this part of the Rainbow Flash. With Sam's help who knows what we might find. Let's stay for a little while."

Bobbie Bear replied, "That would not be the smart thing to do. Large parts of the Rainbow Flash have been explored, which explains my lack of enthusiasm about coming here. We got captured, and you almost got killed. We should leave while we can and return to places where we have a better understanding of the dangers and opportunities."

Randolph yawned and argued, "Yeah, maybe, but hey, it's been a tough few days being stuck in that miserable cage with that awful television going day and night. I really want to take some time to rest and explore. Besides, we got here without having to visit the Grumpy Old Man."

Sam laughed and asked, "Who's the Grumpy Old Man? That's quite a name."

Randolph explained, "The Grumpy Old Man is, well, he's really, really grumpy. Talk about a bad attitude. But if you bring him a problem he usually gives you a solution, or at least a direction to start your search."

"Can you bring him any kind of problem?" Sam asked, thrilled at the idea.

Randolph Coyote the Third answered, "He's pretty good with personal problems and finding things. He's usually right, but not always."

Sam immediately wondered if the Grumpy Old Man might have a solution to his fear of the slide, the swings, and almost everything else. *It certainly would be great, not to feel threatened by so many things,* he thought.

"Can I go see the Grumpy Old Man?" Sam asked.

"Why, you got a problem?" Randolph replied.

"Well, no, but if you're going to take me through a flash anyway, I'd like to see if he's as good as you say. How do I get there?"

"We would have to give you a ride," Bobbie Bear stated.

"Give me a ride? On what?" Sam asked.

Randolph and Bobbie Bear looked at each other and smiled.

"Show him," Bobbie Bear suggested.

Randolph slowly lifted off the bed and floated in the air. He moved his legs as though ambling through the air, glided into the middle of the room and just stood there, about three feet off the ground.

Sam immediately suspected a trick, so he pushed down on Randolph's back. The coyote moved down a little then bobbed up to his original altitude. Randolph and Bobbie Bear chuckled as Sam ran his hands under Randolph's paws and over his back in search of a device, but found nothing. Finally, Sam conceded, "That is too cool. How do you do it?"

Randolph shrugged and said, "Same as talking—I just can."

Randolph's big ears swiveled around. He turned his head toward the door and dropped to the floor just before Sam's mom poked her head in to say dinner would be ready in a minute.

Sam told her OK, and she left, closing the door on her way out.

"Hop on my back. I'll give you a ride around the room," he offered.

"No way," Sam protested. "What if I fall off?"

For years, Sam had written stories about riding on flying animals. He'd even drawn pictures of them, but facing the reality scared him much more than using the slide or the swings at school.

Bobbie Bear explained to Sam, "Do not worry, you

will not fall off. I suggest you try it. Flying is something he does very well. All you have to do is hang on."

Reluctantly Sam swung one leg over Randolph's back, and settled his weight on Randolph's shoulders. The coyote's body felt hard and powerful to Sam, like thick fur covering solid steel.

Randolph lifted about five feet off the ground. He padded gently in a small circle, and suggested to Sam, "If it will make you feel safer, wrap your legs around me and lock your ankles under my chest for a better grip."

Sam held on to Randolph's fur with all his might. His mind filled with thoughts of falling off, breaking his neck, and being paralyzed for life. But he also felt hope that he could be like every other kid. To change, he knew he would have to fly on Randolph's back, so he hung on until they were out of time.

As soon as Sam's mom called, "Dinner," Randolph gently landed. Sam leaped off and fled to the kitchen. A torrent of emotions raged inside Sam during dinner. He sat at the table amazed at the abilities of his new dog and teddy bear, but at the same time, terrified. Writing about flying on Danger Dog had produced no fear in him, but riding on Randolph certainly had.

When the initial shock began to wear off, he thought about what would happen if his new friends thought of him as a scaredy cat. They would not only refuse to take him to the Grumpy Old Man, but they would lose interest in him and leave. He decided that if he got scared he wouldn't show it.

After being excused from the dinner table, Sam raced to his room to find Randolph standing in front of the mirror. The coyote bared his teeth at his reflection and raised the fur on his back. He checked himself out from various angles, grinned, and whispered, "You the dawg!"

Bobbie Bear sat quietly reading a story in one of the books from Sam's big stack, a story set in the time when the English navy worked to rid the Caribbean of pirates. Bobbie Bear asked, "Do you mind if I read this? It is very interesting."

Randolph turned to Sam and added, "Oh, hey, could you also get us some newspapers and magazines? That would be great."

Sam thought that if he could keep them interested they might stay.

"Sure, it's OK to read my books," Sam said. "And I'll get some newspapers and magazines, too. But how did you two learn to read? Don't tell me you just can."

Bobbie Bear replied, "No, we had to learn. When we were held in that cage for three days with the television on all the time, there were captions running under the person speaking. They also lined our cage with newspaper, so we were able to decipher your written language."

Randolph added, "We learned all kinds of cool stuff about your culture. For instance, we found out about Hooligan Harry's Hair House, for fashionable felons. Is that where you go for haircuts?"

"No," Sam said with a laugh.

Bobbie Bear stated with great certainty, "When you have gas you should get CowCalmer pills from Mother Gaspass. Strong enough for a cow, but gentle enough for you. Mother Gaspass, the first name in flatulence."

Sam shook his head and sighed, "Oh, brother!"

The three of them laughed.

Sam went to the living room and came back with an armful of newspapers and magazines, along with three of the books his mother used to become a hospital administrator. He hadn't the foggiest notion what the books were about, but they were the three easiest to grab.

Randolph saw the picture on the front of a local newspaper and pointed out to Sam, "Look, there's a picture of a dog being tortured! See, letting everyone know that we can talk is a bad idea. This is a very dangerous place."

Sam looked at the newspaper, smiled, and explained, "They aren't torturing the dog. The kids are giving him a bath. He'll come out clean and smelling nice."

"You mean he'll come out smelling different from when he went in?"

"Yes."

"That's terrible! If he smells different, how will anyone know who he is?"

Sam grinned and shrugged.

Bobbie Bear flipped through a magazine and asked, “We saw these things on television. This is a picture of an airplane?”

“Yes.”

“And that is how you fly?”

“Yes, it’s the only way we can fly.”

Bobbie Bear and Randolph Coyote the Third looked at each other and burst out laughing. Then Randolph asked Sam, “Hey, you wanna do some real flying outside tonight?”

Despite his terror, he tried to sound courageous when he said, “We’ll have to wait until my parents are asleep. They always come in to check on me before they go to bed, and if I’m missing they’ll freak out.”

“It is very nice that they check up on you,” Bobbie Bear commented.

“I hadn’t thought of it that way, but yeah, I guess it is,” Sam agreed. He took out his homework and tried to concentrate despite his excitement about the approaching adventure. Glancing up from time to time, he saw a coyote and a teddy bear reading newspapers, magazines, and books. He thought, *This is kind of cool. But if my mom saw it, she’d freak.*

Just then Sam’s mom opened the door and poked her head in. Sam spun around in a panic, certain that his new friend’s secret had been revealed.

She smiled and said, "That's so smart of you to put newspapers down on the floor in case the dog makes a mess. Oh, and look at the teddy bear! How cute—you put a book in his lap."

"*Her* lap, Mom."

"Of course, dear. Half an hour to lights out. Don't forget to floss and brush your teeth."

"OK, Mom," Sam replied as she closed the door.

When they were sure she couldn't hear, all three of them broke out laughing.

Chapter 5. Randolph & Bobbie Bear Meet

"Now will you tell me what a flash is?" Sam asked his new friends.

"A flash is a portal between worlds," explained Bobbie Bear. "When you enter a flash, you see a blinding flash of light of a certain color or combination of colors., There are millions of worlds, and each has an entrance, or flash, that has a different combination of colors. Your world, like millions of others, is so far from the center that you see a huge number of colors when you enter it. For convenience, rather than spell out all the colors in your flash, we say you live in the Rainbow Flash."

"So how come I've never heard of all these worlds and our scientists haven't found this flash thing?"

Bobbie Bear shrugged. "I do not know, but finding one is not easy. Flashes are very small and high up in the sky. They can only be seen through a special lens. You have to be at exactly the right place at the right time, and you have to be very close or you cannot see them."

"What happens if you aren't in the right place and

miss one?"

"Nothing awful. You just have to wait for another flash to appear. Sometimes we wait a few minutes, other times days or weeks. Randolph hates missing them, though. Most of the time I can predict which flash will appear and when, but sometimes we have to wait months for the next usable flash that will take us to where we want to go. Usually we must go through several flashes to get to our desired destination."

Sam asked, "Did you two come from the same world? Is that how you met?"

Bobbie Bear and Randolph laughed. Using body language, they urged each other to tell their story. Randolph began:

"No, we come from different worlds. I'm from a world where flying coyotes who can talk like humans exist but are rare. And I could not only speak the way humans do, but sing like them, too. But I was a stupid pup. While I was still quite young, I challenged the best howler in our tribe to a howling contest, certain that my singing ability would carry me to victory. In fact, I felt so sure I'd win that I offered a very big prize—three hundred pounds of meat, enough for the winner's whole family to feast on.

"On the next night of a full moon, warm with the scent of summer in the air, the entire tribe gathered in a clearing for the contest. I went first. I poured myself into performing every howl and song I knew. When I finished, my opponent howled. My heart sank as he performed the best howl I had ever heard—a long one that conveyed terror, tragedy, triumph, beauty, and wonder.

"Of course, a majority voted for him, even two of my own cousins. His howl touched us all so deeply even I would have voted for him. After the voting, his family surrounded me and demanded their three hundred pounds of meat. I knew I had better escape quickly because I would never be able to produce that much meat. My hunting skills weren't very good back then.

"I couldn't fly very well either, so I took a big hop up and over the family. After landing, I headed for the dark woods nearby, with them hot on my heels. I raced over the soft mud of valleys and the hard rocks of hills, through the flower-scented air, under the pitiless gaze of the moon.

"I stayed ahead of them by making big, flying hops. At first, they ran after me because they were angry, but after a few miles they spread out, no longer simply chasing me but hunting me with determination. I was terrified that their fierce eyes might be the last thing I saw.

"All that running left me so tired I could no longer make big, ground-eating hops. They began to close in on me, snapping their fangs at my hind paws. Just then the strangest thing happened. In a small meadow surrounded by trees, I saw ahead of me a wooden wall with an open door. I dashed through it.

"Right away, the hideous smell of the room hit me

but I didn't care. I stood at the door with my tongue hanging out, exhausted and gasping. I watched as my pursuers stopped at the door, sniffed around, and trotted away. As I stood there panting, other dogs' voices from every direction begged me to scurry back out the doorway as fast as possible. Before I had a chance to move the door slammed shut, and the big room began to move. I had vamoosed but became trapped on a ship!"

"Wait a minute. How could a ship operate in the middle of the woods?" Sam asked.

Randolph explained, "Where we come from, ships can sail the seas when they have to, but mostly they fly, so they can land anywhere."

"The way you can fly?" Sam asked.

"Sort of," he remarked and continued his story. "I heard the sound of crude laughter in the dark all around me. Someone lit a lantern, and I could see hundreds of dogs locked up in cages. Instantly I knew that awful smell meant I had jumped into a ship of giant green dog munchers! I tried to escape by flying, but those smelly munchers shut all the hatches. They eventually caught me and threw me in a cage. When the other dogs and I talked, I found out we were all on our way to the muncher's dog food festival."

Sam said, "That sounds great. Lots of dog food for you."

"No, you don't understand," he replied. "Munchers

eat dogs. That's what they do at their dog food festival. And escape became more unlikely by the hour, since we went through many flashes as the munchers visited other worlds to capture more dogs. I didn't know which flash led to my home world, or how to get back.

"When we landed at the muncher's world, they took me out of the filthy, stinking ship's cage and stuffed me into a filthy, stinking cage on land to be fattened for the festival. The munchers fastened a chain around my neck and attached the other end to a boulder to prevent me from flying away in case I got out of the cage. At least once a day, a few munchers would stop by my cage and poke me with a stick to see if I had gained enough fat to make a tasty meal. They laughed when they discussed how they would cook me, and what kind of sauce they would use on me. And in that beastly hot cage in midsummer, I already felt cooked. That's when I met Bobbie Bear."

Bobbie Bear spoke next. "Creatures like me that run on crystals are custom built for wealthy people and serve special needs. For example, they can order a crystal-powered rhinoceros to transport large sums of money, or a crystal--driven dragon to guard a house.

"The company that makes most crystal creatures built me. The company is called Crystal Creature Fabrication Systems or CCFS. They built me as a demonstration model, so I received many abilities, far more than the average crystal creature. I labored at CCFS for two long decades, performing humiliating tricks to impress potential customers. I worked directly with the president and founder of CCFS, the conceited Malcolm Talcum. Middle age had overtaken Mr. Talcum when we first met, and as the years went by he spent more and more time and energy trying to stay young. In the end, he almost never left his private gym and took up bizarre rituals to keep old age at bay, like walking backward thinking that would cause his personal clock to run backward and make him younger.

"The odious Mr. Talcum would pretend that in his youth he had had certain experiences. He claimed to have been a cowboy, a general, a descendant of royalty, and a ship's captain. Every time he came up with a new fake background, his private library would expand with objects that fit his story. He had western saddles, regal coats of arms, and books on the subject, all of them unread by Mr. Talcum. I never received permission to leave the CCFS campus, but at night I had the run of headquarters, including Mr. Talcum's extensive private library. There I read hundreds of books about sailing between the worlds. I read one book after another about life aboard freighters, especially the big long-haul ships that took voyages to dozens of distant worlds. I practiced with the navigation equipment Mr. Talcum had bought in his captain phase.

"One day a great commotion swept through the company. I learned that Mr. Talcum had died. He had choked to death on a vitamin pill while screaming at one of his employees. His death caused so much tumult that the usual rules were ignored for a short time, during which I simply left the campus.

"I walked to the nearest port and obtained a job as a dishwasher on a freighter, the *Mary O. Sole,* finest ship ever to sail the seas and skies. I loved everything about sailing, even the hard work and the danger, but I especially loved learning about navigation. During my time off I would haunt the chart room, where the officers were kind enough to teach me what they knew. Once, the ship even employed a gnome to help navigate a particularly difficult passage. Gnomes are no smarter than other creatures, but they live for many hundreds of years. As a result, they can devote their first hundred years to study and the next hundred to apprenticeship, before beginning a long career in navigation. It is very expensive to hire gnomes, and only the big, long-haul freighters can afford them. The gnome on our freighter taught me a great deal, including advanced navigation and languages and customs of far-off worlds, for which I will always be grateful.

"On one of our journeys we stopped at Bucket Bay, a port famous for attracting evil characters. I decided to remain on board. We rode at anchor three days in the middle of the harbor when a semaphore message arrived saying the harbormaster urgently needed to talk to our captain. I signaled back that the captain had business at the freight company office and told them to go there. They signaled that they could not find our captain there and demanded that I find him. So, I went ashore and headed for the freight company office, but it was a ruse and I never made it. As soon as I passed a particularly dark alley, Yechs abducted me. Yechs are unscrupulous thieves who will grab anything they think will make them money. They brought me to the muncher's world and sold me as a toy for a muncher child. This is really a death sentence because muncher children are notoriously tough on their toys. The muncher who purchased me from the Yechs rushed about organizing the dog food festival that would start the next day. He yelled at his fellow munchers and used me as a club. Finding me an unsatisfactory weapon, since I did not inflict enough damage, he then picked up a real club but needed a handy place to store me for a few hours. He tossed me in Randolph's cage and trudged off to attend to his duties of yelling and clubbing. And that is how Randolph and I met."

Randolph Coyote the Third and Bobbie Bear both laughed at the memory.

Bobbie Bear continued, "So Randolph and I talked about our plight, and I came up with an escape plan."

"*You* came up with it? *I* came up with it," Randolph insisted.

"C'mon, guys, what happened?" Sam asked.

Randolph Coyote the Third went on. "We figured out a simple plan. We would wait until it got good and dark. Then Bobbie Bear would take the chain off my neck, and I would fly straight up, lifting the cage and Bobbie Bear. Once I had lifted the cage, we'd fly to the woods, whack the cage against a tree or rock, shatter it, and escape. But it didn't work out like that."

Bobbie Bear added, "We expected to fly a short distance, break the cage open, and fly off. But there were two cages on top of ours, each with a heavy dog in it, and many more cages on either side."

Randolph continued, "I flew straight up as hard as I could, lifting our cage and the two cages on top of us, but I hadn't reached my full strength because I was so young. Man, I can still remember that load. Heavy! Besides, smoke from the muncher's cook fires filled the inside of the cage, so I could hardly breathe. I could only move the cage a tiny bit at first. I flew straight up and rocked from side to side. The two cages on top of ours and those on either side tumbled to the ground and sprang open. The freed dogs went scooting off in all directions."

Bobbie Bear added, "Yes, all of them stupidly barking, which alerted the munchers to our attempted escape."

Randolph continued, "After the other cages fell off ours, I could only get ours about twenty feet in the air before feeling dog tired. Finally, I spotted the boulder I had been chained to and flew straight down as fast as I could. I smashed into it, causing a huge BANG!"

"We got smashed, as well. My insides became badly

disorganized," Bobbie Bear added.

"Hey, we were going to die anyway. So, we lay stunned in the cage, not feeling too good. After that big crash, I expected the cage would be wrecked, but it looked unharmed. The door and lock were as good as ever, so we still couldn't get out, but that crash did manage to break the chain. All the munchers who had heard that bang started running toward us. Bobbie Bear yelled in my ear, 'Fly! Fly!'"

Bobbie Bear added, "A howling pack of heavily armed munchers ran toward us. Randolph lifted the cage as much as he could, and we hopped along toward the woods inside the cage by going up, forward, down, ka-bang, up, forward, down, ka-bang. It sounds funny now, but we were not laughing then. Finally, after about ten ka-bangs the cage fell apart. We shot out of it and into the woods chased by a flurry of muncher arrows aimed straight at our rears.

"Randolph and I have been traveling together ever since. I do the navigating, and Randolph does the flying," Bobby Bear said.

Randolph said, "We're looking for my home world, but we're not working very hard at it. Members of my tribe have long memories, and they're probably still waiting for their three hundred pounds of meat. Besides, we've been distracted a lot on the way. We just try to have fun wher-ever we are and learn as much as we can about the new worlds we see."

"Wow!" Sam said. He decided their real adventures were a hundred times better than all the stories he had ever read or created. He desperately wanted to have adventures like those, and just as desperately wanted Randolph and Bobbie Bear to be his friends. Sam resolved that he would not let a little thing like fear get in his way, though he found it a hard resolution to keep.

Chapter 6. First Flight

Later that night, while Sam's parents slept, Randolph woke Sam and said, "Hey, get up, man. Let's go flying. If you're gonna go through a flash with us, you gotta get used to a few things. Dress warm, it'll be cold and windy."

Sam instantly went from asleep and relaxed to awake and afraid, but he refused to show his worry. He numbly nodded and squeaked out, "OK" as he pulled on a pair of pants he used for sailing, yellow waterproof overalls, over his pajamas. He put on a pair of elaborately embroidered snow boots his mother had bought at a yard sale, though they were far too big for him. Next, he slipped into his father's ratty old blue tweed sport jacket that Sam had borrowed for a school play. He put on his dad's trooper hat, lowering the earflaps and pulling the strap tight under his chin. When he looked at himself in the mirror, he realized he shouldn't wear a sport jacket without a tie. He dug through his drawers and came up with a purple and green clip-on bow tie, which he affixed to the collar of his pajama tops.

While Sam dressed, Bobbie Bear reached into a pouch in her belly, pulled out a leather harness, and put it on Randolph.

A moment later Sam turned to Bobbie Bear and Randolph and asked, "Is this OK?"

After a long silence, Bobbie Bear replied, "Um, well, I have never seen anything like it."

"Me neither," Randolph quickly agreed.

Eager to change the subject, Bobbie Bear said to Sam, "Kindly open the window as far as it will go."

Sam opened the window. His hands shook from both fear and cold.

Bobbie Bear reached into the pouch again and pulled out three sets of old-fashioned goggles. She put one pair on Randolph, one on herself, and gave the third to Sam. "Here, this is my backup pair. They will protect your eyes from the wind. We will not be going near a flash tonight, but when we do, if you look through the right lens, you will be able to see a flash. The left lens broke, and we could only afford to replace it with ordinary glass. The goggles are perfectly usable otherwise," she said as she climbed onto Randolph's back and slipped her legs under the leather straps. Sam sat behind her, shivering.

"Are you OK?" Randolph asked him.

"Yeah, just cold," Sam managed to mutter as he took off his hat, put on the goggles, put his hat back on, and cinched the chin strap extra tight. His legs held Randolph in a death grip, and he clutched the harness with all his might.

Randolph lifted off the floor and slipped silently out the window. Once clear of the house, he rose about twenty feet, about three times the height of a tall man, and gently strode through the air in a path that took them around Sam's backyard. Randolph announced, "Ladies and gentlemen, welcome aboard Flight One of Dog Air. Please be certain your butt is in an upright and locked position."

Sam laughed nervously and joked, "I've got to keep you guys away from television." He trembled with fear being up that high. Looking at his feet, he saw nothing under them but the hard ground far below. His breath came in short gasps. To control his fear, Sam focused all his attention on the back of Randolph's head. As a result, Sam could not have reported any details of the flight but he could describe in detail the thick tan and gray fur on the back of Randolph's neck.

Sam stood it for as long as he could, his mind filled with gruesome thoughts of falling and having his arms and legs paralyzed. Finally, he begged, "Let me down! Let me down!"

Randolph landed softly next to Sam's mom's rose garden. Sam rolled off and collapsed on the ground. Thinking back, he compared the easy grace of the tiny green insects' flight, as he remembered it from that afternoon, with his own terror-stricken efforts.

Randolph trotted into the rose garden, sniffed around, and lifted his leg against a rosebush. Bobbie Bear crossed her arms, shook her head in disapproval, and asked, "Must you do that everywhere we go?"

"Hey, it's what I do," Randolph said.

Sam felt better after resting for a few minutes. He forced himself to climb on again. Randolph, Bobbie Bear, and Sam lifted off, this time to an altitude of about four times the height of the tallest telephone pole, and Randolph padded silently over the town. This wasn't at all what Sam had imagined flying to be like. He had always thought flying would be fun and make him feel free, but real flying froze him to the bone, making his breath come in rapid gasps. He also found that the waterproof overalls were a poor choice, since they made him slip around on Randolph's back.

Even so, he couldn't help but enjoy the beauty of the scene below. Moonlight bathed his town and the surrounding countryside. The lights of the container port on the other side of the bay twinkled like carefully aligned stars. The view of his town fascinated Sam. From this altitude, his house, his friends' houses, the hardware store, the gas station, his school, and the boat docks all looked very different. When he stood on the ground, he saw the sides of things, like the walls of buildings or the trunks of trees. But gazing straight down he saw roofs and the tops of trees. That made familiar objects look like things he'd never seen before.

Distances looked different, too. When he rode his bike, he knew the exact length of each street. Now, when he looked down on the streets, some were shorter than he thought, and some longer. One part of the river looked closer to the bay, and another part seemed farther away. Although he had lived in this town all his life, he got confused several times and couldn't figure out where they were.

Randolph increased their altitude to five thousand feet, about five times the height of the Empire State Building, and just hung there, moving with the wind as it carried them along. For the first time in Sam's life, the things he dreamed up in his head paled in comparison to the fantastic, amazing, and terrifying things happening in reality.

Finally, Sam pleaded, "Randolph, that's enough. Let me down."

Randolph agreed, "OK, we'll go home. But first we're gonna do one more thing."

Sam screamed in terror as Randolph swooped down and began trotting in a big arc until they were lined up with the highway.

When they were about two hundred feet above the interstate, Randolph leveled off and began running even faster. The button on Sam's sport jacket popped off, making the jacket flap wildly in the wind.

As he ran, Randolph mimicked the voice of a radio announcer: "Welcome to everybody's favorite game show, 'Fly That Dog!' Today's lucky contestant is ... Sam! Bobbie Bear, tell us the fabulous prize Sam has won!"

"Randolph, Sam has won an amazing trip to the interstate!" Bobbie Bear exclaimed. "He will visit the road of song and legend, an unforgettable trip that he will remember for a lifetime, only available here on 'Fly That Dog!'"

Sam laughed, grateful that his new friends were trying to make the experience less scary for him by joking. Sam looked down at the highway and saw a red sports car passing all the other vehicles. Randolph matched the sports car's speed, pulled far ahead, and howled in triumph, "AhhOoooooooooo!"

They raced along the highway and passed every vehicle they saw. Sam wanted to howl along with Randolph, but fear kept him from totally filling his lungs, despite the rush of air hitting his face.

Randolph gained altitude again, to nearly three thousand feet (about three times the height of the Empire State Building) and immediately headed to Sam's house. There, to Sam's great relief, they descended slowly and flew through his open window. Sam collapsed on the floor. He had just enough strength left to hand the goggles back to Bobbie Bear, pull off the sport jacket, pants, snow boots and bow tie, and climb into bed. Randolph and Bobbie Bear flew back out the window to continue their explorations.

Sam tried to calm down and come to grips with what had just happened. He had experienced the most amazing adventure, one far more daring than his friends had ever encountered on the playground. Flying Randolph had been terrifying, but, in retrospect, also fun. He had the courage to fly on the back of a huge coyote thousands of feet up in the air, going faster than any sports car. His success left him feeling shaken yet proud of himself. Sam thought about his imaginary hero Danger Dog and smiled. He now realized that the pretend adventures of Danger Dog seemed silly after the real adventure of flying with Randolph and Bobbie Bear.

As Sam drifted off to sleep, he softly sang:

A dog, a dog, I got the greatest dog.
I've found his name is hardly Spot.
Dread gripped my heart, but fear I
fought.
I might get courage 'cause I got
A dog, a dog, a dog.

Chapter 7. Setting a Course

At breakfast the next morning, while his dad read the newspaper and his mom studied a report for work, Sam told them about his adventure the night before. Without taking his eyes off the newspaper, his dad mumbled, "Finish your breakfast or you'll be late for school."

At recess, Sam tried to tell his classmate Howard that his new dog could fly and talk. Howard shook his head and said, "Yeah, right. When I see him fly and talk, I'll believe it." Howard ambled off to play on the monkey bars.

That night Sam asked his new friends, "Could I bring you guys to show-and-tell? My friend Howard doesn't believe I have a flying talking dog."

Bobbie Bear explained patiently, "Randolph and I have discussed that very issue. We do not think it is a good idea. If we were to display our abilities, word would spread quickly and people from your world would demand answers. They would insist on knowing where we come from, or, at the very least, make educated guesses about our origins. They would learn that flashes exist and would quickly figure out how to use them to visit other worlds."

"Not that we've got anything against folks from your world," Randolph added. "From what we've seen so far they're no better or worse than any other bunch. But we have something called the Inter-Flash Council. They're the ones who let a world in on flashes, or keep them out. They do other stuff too, like standardize navigation, settle trade disputes between worlds, and all that. Anyway, if, without the Council's OK, someone lets the people of a world know about flashes and how to use them the Council gets hopping mad. They throw guys in jail for life for doing stuff like that."

Bobbie Bear continued, "So, sadly, we must decline your kind invitation to, um . . ."

"Show-and-tell," Sam said. He added in a dejected tone, "You guys probably won't even take me through a flash."

"Way not true, dude. A deal's a deal. We fly tonight!" Randolph exclaimed. "We're gonna go through a flash or two and visit the Grumpy Old Man. It's gonna be cold up there, so dress warm."

"OK," Sam answered in a shaky voice. He tried to sound nonchalant and hide his terror, but he wasn't doing a very good job. For this flight Sam put on a pair of heavy wool pants, sturdy hiking boots, a wool shirt and thick sweater, his father's yellow waterproof jacket that was too big for him, and the goggles Bobbie Bear handed him. He put on his trooper hat, pulled down the ear flaps and fastened the strap tight under his chin. He pulled the hood of his jacket up over his hat as a finishing touch to his outfit.

He felt better prepared this time but still nervous. "What if we go through a flash and can't get back?" he stammered.

Randolph explained, "We'll get back. Bobbie Bear is a very good navigator. When we escaped from the muncher's world, we were bounced around so hard that Bobbie's navigation equipment stopped working. But she figured out how to make a sextant from a flat piece of board, a string, and a weight. She also created a compass from a little magnet we found in a trash heap. Her equipment didn't work well, but it worked, and she got us out of there. And I happen to be excellent at flying. We've done this many times together."

"You sure I won't get you guys in trouble with those Inter-Flash Council guys?" Sam asked.

Randolph replied, "Naw, you're just a kid who makes up stories. If you told everyone all about flashes and how to use them, no one would believe you. But to be on the safe side, and to keep people in other flashes from asking embarrassing questions, when we're in other worlds tell anyone who asks that you're from the Blue-Green-Yellow Flash. Got that?"

"Blue-Green-Yellow, Blue-Green-Yellow, Blue-

Green-Yellow," Sam murmured to himself to lock the words in his mind.

Bobbie Bear said to Sam, "Randolph is correct. By bringing you through, we could run afoul of the Inter-Flash Council's rules, but that possibility is remote. However, I should point out that it is not necessary for you to go on this journey. There is a chance that the Grumpy Old Man may not be able to help you, and I am not sure you are sufficiently prepared to ride Randolph if he makes a run for a flash."

Randolph added, "But if you don't try, you'll never know what you can do. Besides, going from one world to another is pretty cool."

Sam took a deep breath and said, "OK, let's go!"

"Yes!" Randolph answered, glad to see Sam set to try. "Let's get ready!"

Bobbie Bear opened a secret pocket on her belly. To Sam it looked like a kangaroo's pouch until he peered inside and saw eight small instruments, each with many hands, along with tiny switches and dials neatly set into a dark wood panel. The only instruments Sam recognized were five small compasses, but they had both horizontal and vertical compass cards.

Sam asked, "What is all that?"

"This is my navigation equipment. It is necessary for me to set these instruments before we take off to ensure that we can get back here."

"Good idea. And what's that thing on the side?" Sam asked, pointing to the small instrument.

Bobbie removed it and handed it to Sam. "That is a three-dimensional sextant used for navigation between the worlds. It is a very small one, but it works reasonably well."

Bobbie took out a flat square of brass with many markings engraved on both sides and circles of brass riveted to it so that they could rotate freely. She added, "This is a course calculator. By rotating these circles to match marks on other circles, I can calculate our course. It takes the place of several hundred pounds of almanacs. It's not quite as good as an almanac, but it can be carried easily and will get us quite close to our destination."

Sam's opinion of Bobbie Bear rose a great deal. He examined the tiny brass sextant gleaming in his hand. It looked like three normal sextants bound together, with gears, cams, and shafts running from each one to the other two so that an adjustment of any sextant affected them all.

Sam gently touched the cool, smooth instrument, delighted by its complexity. He thought the craftsmanship of the tiny sextant surpassed any he had seen before at the local maritime museum. He thought using it would be fun.

Sam handed the sextant back to Bobbie Bear, looked inside her pouch, and asked, "What are those two things?"

Bobbie Bear took them out and showed them to

Sam, who said, "You carry salt and pepper shakers?"

Randolph Coyote the Third laughed and said, "Yeah, give your friends a thrill. Put a little of that 'salt' on their fries."

Bobbie Bear giggled at the thought, and replied, "This is not salt and that is not pepper. This one is white pixie pollen, and that is black pixie pollen. Flashes are very small, about the size of a penny. We use the white pollen to shrink us down to get through a flash, and the black to bring us back to our original size. I sprinkle a bit of the white stuff on us and we shrink, and then a bit of the black stuff and we expand with no trouble at all."

"How does it work?" Sam asked.

"That's a good question. No one knows, but we do know one thing," Randolph said. "The pixies are the only ones who can produce it, and they charge plenty. If you want to get from one world to another—no pixie pollen, no go."

"If it's so expensive, how do you pay for it?"

"We have jobs," Randolph revealed, somewhat indignantly.

"What do you do?"

"Remember when we first met your mother? How Randolph tossed me in the air and caught me on his snout? Randolph and I are a featured act with the Alakzoo-tle, Tweedle and Tootle Circus and Sideshow Suprimo. We do tumbling and gymnastics. I also work in the office and as a ticket taker and barker. We both help set up and take down the tents. That is mostly how we earn money."

The unexpected news delighted Sam. "You two are circus performers?!"

Randolph huffed, "We are not performers. We're stars! We travel all the known worlds, and are greeted with headlines and top billing wherever we go."

"Wow."

Sam noticed that the pixie pollen shakers were only about a quarter full. "Is there enough?" he asked.

"For this trip we have more than enough, but we need to start thinking about obtaining more," Bobbie Bear replied, and went back to setting her instruments.

The professional way Bobbie Bear handled her instruments and the knowledge that she and Randolph traveled a great deal among the worlds reassured Sam. Though he still felt mostly fear, he now believed that Bobbie Bear and Randolph Coyote the Third could get him there and bring him back.

Something suddenly occurred to Sam, and he said, "How long will this trip take? Remember, we have to be back before my parents wake up. That's only a few hours from now."

"Don't worry about that," Randolph said. "Time runs at different rates in different flashes. It runs very slowly in your world, so we'll have plenty of time."

After Bobbie Bear finished setting her navigation

equipment, she began packing items for the trip. She went to the kitchen and took a big bag of freshly baked cookies. When she returned to Sam's room, she grabbed one of Sam's mom's paperback books, a volume on finance. She stuffed it into a waterproof pocket in Sam's jacket as he finished dressing.

Bobbie Bear reached into her pouch and pulled out the sets of goggles. Sam put his on while Bobbie Bear helped Randolph.

Sam opened the window with trembling hands, and thought to himself:

This is nuts, I can't believe I'm going.
Off to some place there simply is no knowing.
Flying a dog? This is totally absurd.
What am I thinking, that this mutt's really a bird?

With shaky knees Sam followed Bobbie Bear's instructions to take the bag of cookies, sit on Randolph's shoulders, and hang on.

Randolph asked Sam, "You OK?"

"Yeah," Sam answered, although his teeth chattered with fear.

Hearing Sam's teeth and feeling him shiver, Bobbie Bear suggested, "Randolph, I think we should cancel this. Sam seems scared out of his wits."

"Aw, once we get some altitude he'll love it. Besides,

all he has to do is hang on. What's the worst that can happen?" Randolph replied.

"That is what I am considering. We should at least postpone a flight through a flash."

Randolph asked Sam, "Hey, kid, you up for this?"

Through a fog of terror, Sam grunted, "Uh-huh" as he looked around his room. This could be the last time he would ever see his room or his home. He studied the walls and floor, greedily memorizing every detail.

Randolph instructed, "Just remember, Sam, relax and think of this as nothing but fun. Oh, and if you tie the bag of cookies to your belt, it will be one less thing to worry about."

As soon as Sam finished tying the bag of cookies to his belt, Randolph lifted off the ground. Sam clamped his legs around the coyote's big chest and held the harness with all his might. Randolph began padding through the air. They slipped silently through the window and out into the vast night sky.

Chapter 8. Navigating a Flash

As they rose swiftly into the sky, Sam couldn't take his eyes off the rapidly shrinking landscape below. He kept thinking, *All I've got between me and death is this coyote! What if he loses his ability to fly? What if I fall off?* Sam clamped his legs tighter around Randolph's chest and held the straps more firmly.

Finally, they stopped gaining altitude and hung in midair, thousands of feet above the ground. Sam looked longingly at the brightly lit container port. He wanted to ask Randolph to forget about flashes and grumpy old men and drop him off where his father worked in the offices that ran the docks, but he forced himself to be silent.

Bobbie Bear told Randolph to hold his position. Randolph pushed against the wind, and they bobbed like a light rowboat in a choppy sea. Bobbie Bear took several sightings with her sextant and worked with the course calculator.

"If we miss this one, how long to the next usable flash?" Randolph asked.

"Eleven days," Bobbie Bear replied. "Sam, do not look down. Look straight ahead or up," she warned Sam.

Sam glanced over Bobbie Bear's shoulder and noticed her navigation instruments glowing softly in the dark. For a moment, his fascination with them took his mind from being scared.

Staring at the instruments, Bobbie Bear told Randolph, "Turn left. More. Stop. Go straight up and forward, more, more, more, slow down, a little more forward, stop there. Now turn to your right very slightly. Perfect. Hold this position. Now we wait."

Bobbie Bear turned to Sam and explained, "We cannot go directly from the Rainbow Flash to the Black-Brown-Black Flash, which is the entrance to the Grumpy Old Man's world. We need to go through the Pink-Green-Red Flash first, where we are much more likely to find the Black-Brown-Black Flash."

Sam nodded as he shivered, not just from fear but from the strong cold wind. Once again, he forced himself to be quiet, although he wanted to say, "Please take me back to my warm bedroom!" He knew that if he said that his new friends would indeed take him back but then leave forever. Sam thought about never flying a coyote again, never going through a flash, never having adventures that were real, just having a lifetime of make-believe adventures, like the Danger Dog stories. He clutched the leather straps and watched Bobbie Bear navigate.

As if reading his thoughts, Bobbie Bear said, "Hang on, Sam. We will have you through the Pink-Green-Red Flash and on solid ground in no time. You will like the world we are about to enter. It is one of the most civilized places in all the known worlds and is famous for its exquisite gardens, divine music, and high level of culture."

"The food is real good, too," Randolph added.

With her eyes fixed on her instruments, Bobbie Bear ordered Randolph, "Turn left, a little more. Good. Now go up, more, more, stop. It is about a mile straight in front of you."

Randolph began a quick trot.

"You are right on it. Go!" prompted Bobbie Bear.

Randolph started running in earnest, every step increasing Sam's fear that he would fall off. Now that Randolph's big chest expanded and contracted rapidly in time with his quick pace, Sam struggled to keep his ankles locked and he tightened his grip on the straps even more.

To take his mind off his fear of falling, Sam strained his eyes to search for the flash. He shouted over the wind to Bobbie Bear, "I don't see anything but a few clouds in the distance."

Bobbie Bear, still watching her instruments as Randolph ran, yelled back, "You will not see it until we are on it, and maybe not even then. It is very small. When we get close, I will use the white pixie pollen. As we get smaller it will appear that the flash gets bigger. You will definitely see it then."

Bobbie Bear took out the shaker with the white pixie pollen and, at exactly the right moment, shook a tiny amount on the three travelers and called out, "White pollen away!"

Sam did not feel himself shrinking, but as he watched the flash he knew he was getting smaller because the portal seemed to be getting bigger.

Sam closed his left eye, then his right. When he looked through the right lens of the goggles he clearly saw the flash, but when he looked only through the left lens he saw nothing but a few moonlit clouds. As Randolph increased his altitude slightly, the flash vanished entirely.

Bobbie Bear yelled over the wind, "Randolph, I think we are too late for this one! Slow down and we will catch the next one!"

But Randolph shouted back, determined, "No way! I'm not gonna waste that pixie pollen, and I'm definitely not gonna wait eleven days. I will get this one!" He increased his pace.

The wind howled in Sam's ears and made his clothes flap. He glanced down and saw that Randolph's legs were a blur as the three of them shot through the night sky.

Looking through the left lens, Sam could see nothing ahead but dark sky and a few clouds. But when he leaned forward so his eyes were on the same level as Randolph's and looked through the right lens, he saw a misty circle of light rapidly approaching.

As they drew closer, Bobbie Bear yelled to Randolph, "We are looking for the Pink-Green-Red Flash. This one looks like a Red-Green-Red Flash. It might be the wrong one!"

"It looks pink to me! You worry too much!" Randolph yelled back as he sped up. "I *will* get this one!"

An updraft increased their altitude slightly, and the flash disappeared. Still, Randolph continued his furious pace, though he dropped down a bit. Sam saw the flash reappear for a moment and then disappear again as Randolph overshot. Finally, Randolph corrected his altitude slightly upward, and the flash reappeared once more.

Bobbie Bear yelled, "I do not think this is the right one. The inside band of color looks red, not pink!"

"Looks pink to me!" Randolph yelled.

Bobbie Bear yelled back, "Not to me! I have no idea what is in the Red-Green-Red Flash. Break off! We have got to wait for the right flash."

"It *is* the right flash and I am not going to wait eleven days! Pink! Pink! Pink! Ah-Oooooow!" Randolph howled as they barreled forward.

The argument between Randolph and Bobbie Bear only increased Sam's fear. Meanwhile, colors moved around in the flash so quickly, and were so vague, that he couldn't determine red, green, or anything else.

Sam yelled to Bobbie Bear, "How can you be sure of the colors of a flash? This one looks like a misty blob with different colors moving around in it."

"It takes time to learn to read them. At first, they looked like that to me too," replied Bobbie Bear.

As they got closer and the view improved, Sam could see that the flash looked like colors pulsing out of the middle of a giant, filmy, nearly transparent flower. Even up close, Sam had so much trouble seeing it that he could now understand why no one in his world knew of flashes. He could also see how a very large ship, shrunk down with pixie pollen, could easily fit through a flash.

When they were very near, Sam noticed a distinct odor in the air, somewhat like the smell of an electrical wire sparking. Fear had been drizzling on Sam like a constant rain, but now that he could see the flash the drizzle turned to a downpour. He wanted to ask if going through a flash hurt, but he didn't, worried that Randolph and Bobbie Bear would think less of him.

Sam leaned back to postpone entering the flash as long as possible. It suddenly occurred to him that he really didn't know anything about Randolph or Bobbie Bear except for the tales they had told him about themselves. They might have been lying the entire time. They might not be taking him to see the Grumpy Old Man. There might not even be such a person. They might be kidnapping him and taking him to cannibals to sell as lunch! Sam leaned back even more.

Sam also realized that his parents could not help him if he got into trouble. They had no idea that, at the moment, he was only a fraction of an inch tall. He clung to the back of an equally tiny flying coyote thousands of feet up in the night sky headed for a weird, pulsing, shimmering circle of light. His parents had told him over and over about the dangers of going off with strangers, but they had never said anything about nonhuman strangers. Sam leaned back even farther, causing the wind to grab the bottom of his jacket and shirt and yank them up to his chest.

Instantly the flash vanished.

Randolph yelled, "Hey, Sam, straighten up! I can't fly with you hanging out the back like that!"

Numbly, Sam followed Randolph's instructions and pushed against the wind until he tilted slightly forward. The cold wind blasted against his bare stomach, but Sam didn't dare release a hand from the straps to pull his shirt and jacket down.

Randolph readjusted his altitude, and the flash reappeared.

Bobbie Bear shouted, "You are dead center, but that still looks red to me!"

"Pink! Pink! Pink!" Randolph shouted back.

As they barreled through the flash, a powerful burst of light hit Sam and he couldn't see a thing.

Chapter 9. Danger in a Different World

Sam blinked in an effort to clear his vision but remained blind for thirty seconds. When his vision returned he slowly began to make out gray mist all around them. They had come out of the flash and into a cloud. Sam felt the cool fog-like moisture soak his face and cover his goggles.

Randolph slowed his pace to a stroll and descended, still breathing hard. Sam sighed with relief. Going through a flash hadn't hurt at all. He had lost his eyesight for about half a minute, similar to what happened when a flashbulb went off while he looked at a camera. However, his vision came right back and he had experienced no pain.

Sam pulled his shirt and jacket down to cover his stomach, wiped his goggles with his hand and turned around to look at the flash. What he thought he saw looked like a purple, blue, and red flash behind them as it quickly broke apart and faded into nothingness.

Bobbie Bear took out the shaker with the black pixie pollen and gave it a slight jiggle as they continued to descend. Once again, Sam felt no difference.

"Hey, Bobbie, it's not the same," he commented.

"What is not the same?" Bobbie Bear asked.

"The flash we came out of. It seemed like we went into a Red-Green-Red Flash, but we came out of one that looked sort of purplish," Sam said, worrying about getting back.

"Yes, that is one reason it is so difficult to navigate between the worlds. If you go through a flash, turn around and go back through it again, you will not return to the place where you began, but instead be somewhere else entirely."

Although Sam could see nothing but mist, he knew they were descending by the upward direction of the wind and the occasional popping in his ears. He could see neither the ground nor the sky, just moist clouds.

Randolph sniffed and complained, "Hey, this isn't the Pink-Green-Red Flash. We are in the wrong place. Bobbie, how come you took us to the wrong place?"

Sam had seen Bobbie Bear be very polite, so he giggled with surprise when she growled and smacked Randolph on the head.

"Ouch!" Randolph yelped.

Bobbie Bear returned to her instruments while muttering to herself.

"Hey, it's pretty nice here though. Interesting smells," Randolph commented, sniffing inquisitively.

As they broke through the cloud cover, Sam breathed in the moist scent of jungle wafting up from the tree canopy below. Within seconds, the air filled with gentle, fat raindrops.

Randolph suggested, “Sam, tip your head back and stick out your tongue, man.”

Sam’s mouth and throat were parched from fear and excitement. The raindrops tasted so clean and sweet that getting soaked didn’t bother him at all.

Despite the rain, Bobbie Bear continued to work with her navigation equipment. As she took a sighting with her sextant, she warned, “Randolph, keep your eyes open. We know nothing about this world, and there is no telling what dangers lurk here.”

“OK, OK,” Randolph spoke the words but ignored Bobbie Bear completely as he continued to lap up raindrops.

Suddenly, the three of them gasped at the sight of a flock of pterodactyls flying just above the treetops.

An enormous snake sprang out of the trees, snatched a pterodactyl in its huge jaws, and slunk below the treetops with its prey furiously struggling in vain to free itself.

The three travelers reacted like sports fans after a great play:

“Whoa, did you see that!”

“Amazing! Amazing!”

“I’ve never witnessed anything like it!”

"What a grab! Right out of the air!"

"The power and speed of that snake, as well as its size, were very impressive."

Randolph quipped, "Too cool, man, but Bobbie Bear might be right. This ain't exactly the sort of family-friendly place you'd want to bring a kid." As soon as Randolph said this, he realized that they had, indeed brought a child to this place. He hung his head a little, but only for a moment.

Finally, the rain stopped and the sky cleared. Sam yelled, "Wow, look!" He pointed at two moons rising in a green sky. "Can we come back here someday?" he pleaded.

Bobbie Bear answered distractedly as she focused on her instruments, "Maybe. I think I can get us back here if that is what you really want." After looking more closely at her instruments, she shook her head in disbelief and declared, "Randolph, I have never understood how you can do stupid things and get brilliant results."

Randolph chuckled. He heard that comment from Bobbie Bear regularly.

Bobbie Bear continued, "Amazingly, the correct flash should be nearby very soon now. As you have just seen, this is a dangerous place. Randolph, eyes open."

Randolph sniffed and commented, "A flash is very close."

Sam sniffed and picked up the distinctive, slightly electrical smell of a flash. He now felt no fear about going through one, and if all the other worlds were this fabulous he couldn't wait to see the next one.

"Go up about a foot. I think we might be incredibly lucky," said Bobbie Bear.

Randolph rose slightly. Sam saw through the right eyepiece of his goggles the tiny, ghostly shape of the flash only a few feet away. Trying to make sense of the colors, he thought he could see some black and brown but wasn't sure.

Bobbie Bear, never taking her eyes off her instruments, shook a little of the white pixie pollen on the three.

Before the white pixie pollen could take effect, Randolph lurched down so fast that Sam almost lost his grip. The speed of the maneuver made Sam's head snap up, and he saw a powerful, leather-winged pterodactyl with fierce yellow eyes swooping down on him, its big claws aimed straight at his chest. Its talons were each the size of Sam's arm. One of them whizzed by his head so close he could feel the wind zip through his hair. He hung on desperately as Randolph unexpectedly changed direction and charged almost straight up.

The pixie pollen began to take effect. As the three shrunk rapidly, Sam looked back and saw the pterodactyl appear to grow much bigger. It turned in a tight circle to make another try. Although they were almost too large to fit, Randolph bounded through.

A wave of terror swept over Sam. They were through the flash, and the fierce pterodactyl no longer posed a threat, but he realized he had very narrowly missed being skewered and eaten.

"That was close," Randolph admitted quietly.

"I had my eyes on my instruments. What happened?" Bobbie Bear asked.

"Pterodactyl. Almost had Sam for lunch."

"Hmm," Bobbie Bear replied, and nodded as she sprinkled them with black pixie pollen.

After Sam calmed down he saw they were hovering above a place where the sun shone dimly. Unlike the sweet air of the last world, the chemical stench here overwhelmed his senses. Through the thick, hazy air, Sam surveyed the scene. He recoiled at the sight of huge, rust-colored factories as far as he could see. Acrid smoke poured from the sooty brick smokestacks. Even at this altitude he clearly heard the clank and roar of machinery. To Sam the steel gray clouds looked like they held up a sagging sky. The ground, buildings, roads, and even the trees seemed to gasp under a thick coat of brown dust. Dark brown soot drizzled from the sky like an evil rain, making him cough and sneeze.

Bobbie Bear declared, "Excellent! Just where we want to be."

Randolph quipped, "Ain't this a lovely place? Lucky we didn't come during tourist season."

Randolph quickly descended to bring Sam to meet the Grumpy Old Man.

Chapter 10. Sam & the Grumpy Old Man

Bobbie Bear examined the Grumpy Old Man's yard and remarked, "Yuck! This place is even worse than the last time we were here!"

The roof of the small, wooden house sagged, and one end of the porch lay collapsed on the ground. A greasy cloud hung overhead, and the wind brought a rotten egg smell from the nearby factory. Many pairs of false teeth littered the yard. The Grumpy Old Man could never find a pair that fit well and routinely tossed the ill-fitting ones out the window. There were also many pairs of old, smelly boots, as well as bits and pieces of broken toasters and TVs.

Randolph instructed Sam, "Knock on the door and tell him what you want."

"Me? Alone?" Sam protested as he climbed off Randolph. His legs were stiff from clamping onto the big coyote.

Bobbie Bear explained, "You are the one who wants

to ask him for a solution to a problem."

"Would one of you come up there with me?"

"No, you gotta do it yourself," said Randolph. "Take the bag of cookies."

Sam didn't like the idea of approaching the Grumpy Old Man alone, but he lumbered, stiff-legged, to the front door and pushed the buzzer. It didn't work, so Sam knocked.

"Go away! Get off my porch! Go on, scram!" came a loud, raspy voice from inside.

Sam fled the porch, his stomach churning with a sense of rejection. He begged Randolph and Bobbie Bear, "Please, let's leave. He's scary and he told me to go away."

"You're just gonna give up?" Randolph asked.

"I guess maybe I shouldn't?" answered Sam, remembering that he had come all this way to learn how to be less scared of everything.

Randolph explained patiently, "The Grumpy Old Man is not pleasant, but he is very good at telling you how to get to what you need. Bobbie Bear and I can't do that, so you have to confront the Grumpy Old Man."

Sam did not want any confrontations with anyone, especially not with the Grumpy Old Man. But he swallowed hard, went up to the door, and knocked a second time.

"I told you to go away! Get off my porch!"

Sam came close to tears, with a feeling of utter

failure. He desperately wanted to be accepted by Randolph and Bobbie Bear, but for that to happen he needed to do something very hard, confront a grown-up who had told him to go away.

He turned and shuffled back to Randolph and Bobbie Bear, who both seemed to have no expression at all, neither smiling nor frowning, neither approving nor disapproving. To Sam they looked like stone gods sitting in judgment, deciding if they wanted him to join them in their adventures or take him home and leave him there forever.

Sam stared at them for what felt like a long time. He hated to give up after coming so far, but the Grumpy Old Man still terrified him. Finally, Sam forced himself to whisper, "Guess I'll try again."

Sam approached the porch with a bottomless pit of dread in his stomach. A grown-up had told him to go away, but, despite that, he stood there meekly on the Grumpy Old Man's porch.

Sam waited for the butterflies in his stomach to stop colliding with each other. When they calmed down a little Sam knocked on the door once again. He hoped the Grumpy Old Man had left on vacation or at least lost his voice from shouting so loudly, but neither had happened.

"I told you to go away! Get out of here!"

Timidly Sam asked, "Would you like some cookies?"

The Grumpy Old Man paused and then bellowed,

"What kind?"

"Oatmeal raisin. They're fresh from the oven."

After a few seconds the Grumpy Old Man shouted, "Throw them through the window."

Sam tossed the bag of cookies through the open window. A moment later a shattering noise assaulted Sam as the Grumpy Old Man crunched through the big pile of cookies, devouring all of them at once.

The Grumpy Old Man let out a huge belch and yelled, "Those weren't as horrible as I thought they'd be. You get to ask one question. What do you want?"

Sam didn't know how to ask his question, but he knew he'd have to do it quickly, so he blurted out, "Well, I go to a really nice school, with a really nice playground . . ."

"What is your question!" he roared impatiently.

Sam jumped. He got to the point, but he whispered so Bobbie Bear and Randolph couldn't hear. "I'm scared a lot. How do I become brave?"

No sound came from the house. Sam feared he would get no answer, but then the Grumpy Old Man shouted, "Fly through Blue-Yellow-Blue. Go north to Thunder Mountain—it's the jagged one. Find a solution to the problem."

"North?"

"Yes, north, as in not south, not east, and not west!" the Grumpy Old Man roared with mounting irritation.

"What solution? What problem?" Sam asked.

"I said one question only!" roared the Grumpy Old Man. "You've asked your question, now get off my porch!"

Randolph and Bobbie Bear motioned for Sam to come back to them.

Bobbie Bear stated with a smile, "You confronted him with determination and got what you needed. Good job, Sam!"

Randolph added, "And the Grumpy Old Man shouted so loud, we heard what he said. Let's go!"

Sam beamed with pride. He said gratefully, "Guys, I really want to thank you for helping me."

Randolph Coyote the Third replied, "Hey, you saved us when we needed it. Besides, all we're about to do is go through a flash and fly north. What could go wrong?"

Sam, Bobbie Bear, and Randolph all put on their goggles and took off. They went through the Blue-Yellow-Blue Flash and headed north, straight into the worst storm any of them had ever encountered.

Chapter 11. Thunder Mountain

As the storm raged around them, Sam clamped his ankles together under Randolph and put his arms through the leather straps of the harness to lock himself in place. Randolph ran on and on. One moment they were bouncing through dark clouds like a tiny speedboat smacking against big waves. The next moment they seemed to be in an elevator gone mad, hurtling down and down with stomach wrenching speed, then up and up as though whacked from below by a giant baseball bat. Sam clutched Randolph with all his strength while they were tossed and battered, yanked and pulled. If this had gone on for only a few minutes, it would have been dreadful enough, but it went on and on and on.

Sam shuddered with fear. Bobbie Bear read the compass as best she could and called out course corrections to Randolph, but their violent gyrations made the compass cards roll and spin. Each time this happened, Bobbie Bear lost track of the direction they were headed. But they flew on like a ping-pong ball lurching its way through a washing machine. The clouds were so thick that midday looked like murky sunset, shattered occasionally by flashes of lightning so sudden and bright they made Sam flinch.

Randolph continued running. Fighting the wind, he seemed unaffected by the explosions of thunder all around him.

Sam thought back to times when he had sat on a bench at school and dreamed up silly characters like Danger Dog. Sam realized that sitting in comfort and safety while imagining flying through storms gave him not the faintest hint of what the real experience felt like.

Bobbie Bear and Randolph surprised Sam by singing:

> The muskrat and the ocelot flew kites on
> windy beaches.
> They ran through dunes and crashing surf
> devouring giant peaches.
> They sang a song of fishermen who toil on
> the sea
> And wrote a note to Mr. Fish inviting him to
> tea.

Sam laughed at the silly words and joined in.

> The capybara danced the hula late one

summer's night.
Her dancing scared the ostrich so he tried
to take to flight.
He ran through crowds of antelope who
calmly knitted socks
And talked about how hard it was to tango
with an ox.

The three of them flew through the storm, wet, cold, and shaken, but singing and laughing.

Randolph ran for what felt to Sam like a long distance when a sudden flash of lightning gave off enough light for Sam to see a mountain in the distance with a round, smooth top. All three felt disappointed but continued on.

A second flash of lightning showed another round, smooth mountain, disappointing the three further.

Soon, instead of running steadily, Randolph started to glide short distances to catch his breath. Sam yelled to him, "If you're too tired to go on, we should stop somewhere and rest, or maybe turn back."

"No way! I will make it!" Randolph insisted.

Finally, another flash of lightning revealed the top of a jagged mountain looming ahead. "That must be Thunder Mountain!" Sam hollered, relieved and excited to see it at last.

Although close to exhaustion, Randolph stopped

gliding and fought against the howling blasts of wind in his struggle to keep them on course for the mountain. Despite a terrific final pounding from the violent storm, Randolph used the last of his strength to crash land on a ledge on the mountain's sheer south Side.

Randolph sat on the hard, cold, wet rock of the ledge, his head and tongue hanging down. He looked wide-eyed at nothing and panted hard for several minutes. Sam felt tired, but Randolph looked debilitated.

Randolph rolled over, lay on his back, opened his mouth and let the cold rain fall into his parched mouth. Sam saw that, thought it was smart, and did the same. Within a few minutes both had had enough to drink.

The wind howled, lightning flashed, thunder rumbled, and the rain poured down in freezing sheets. Sam regretted ever having left his bedroom.

Looking around, he realized they were perched high on a cliff between two enormous caves, one to the east and the other to the west. A narrow path led to the East cave. Sam, noticing that a small stream flowed out of each cave, shouted over the storm's noise, "Randolph, can you fly us to one of the caves for shelter?"

The coyote shook his head wearily and said, "The wind is too strong, and I'm still very tired! We were lucky to land at all. If we try to take off now, we'll be hammered against the rocks. We'll have to wait here until the wind dies down and I can rest a little more."

Sam peered over the edge of the cliff, straight down thousands of feet to swirling clouds and a foaming, churning river below. He backed away from the edge as far as he could. He glanced at Randolph and Bobbie Bear. They seemed oddly content while waiting out the storm.

Randolph soon recovered enough to sniff around the ledge and raise his leg on a rock. He then took several steps north, circled three times, and lay down as close to the cliff as he could.

Bobbie Bear sheltered under Sam's raincoat, pulled the book out of the waterproof jacket pocket, and became absorbed in reading about finance.

"Hey, Sam," Randolph said a few minutes later, "how about you, me, and Bobbie Bear go into the real estate business together? We could bolt hundreds of condos to this rock face. I got a great name for it, too. The Cliffs. Waddaya think? The best part is we don't need any money to do it. We can make millions in real estate with no money down. I saw it on television, so it must be true."

The other two laughed. Randolph sat up and let out a rock shaking "AhhOooooooooo!" His howl echoed from one cliff face to the next until it sounded like a dozen coyotes.

Seeing Randolph back to his old self gave Sam a great sense of relief. But Bobbie Bear warned, "Randolph, do not do that! We do not know who or what is in this place. It is far wiser to keep our presence unknown until you are able to fly."

"Ah, loosen up, Bobbie. There's nothing here to worry about," Randolph replied as he lay down. He fell asleep almost instantly, after which Bobbie Bear went back to her reading.

Sam, cold and miserable, envied the way his two friends made themselves comfortable in such harsh circumstances. Sam jammed himself against the cliff wall to get what shelter and rest he could. But then he saw something astonishing.

Flying out of the West cave were three wooden masts held together with spars and ropes, each mast supporting three square-rigged sails.

A sailor stood in the crow's nest, dressed in a three-cornered hat, a ruffled white shirt, a black vest, black knee-breeches, black shoes with brass buckles, and a large, elaborately embroidered coat. The sailor's shoes gleamed and his clothes looked new and freshly pressed. He sported a long and carefully styled mustache. Sam thought he looked exactly like the pictures of pirates in his storybooks.

The pirate controlled the sails through a series of lines that led to his perch in the crow's nest. Lashed to the masts and spars were small muzzle-loading cannons. At first Sam thought this strange contraption sprang from his imagination. But then he realized that not even he could dream up something like this. He yelled, "Hey guys, look at that!"

Randolph and Bobbie Bear were equally astonished.

To Sam, the arrangement of masts and spars seemed jury-rigged so only the great skill of the pirate could keep them together in high winds. The pirate himself looked lean and fierce. As he swooped by, he gazed at the three friends with razor sharp eyes and laughed at them, the way a hawk might laugh at a mouse just before pouncing in for the kill.

He roared above the wind, "I know you've been sent by that contemptible Mr. Bland! Prepare to meet your doom!"

He fired all his guns.

The cannonballs crashed into the cliff's rock face. They sent stone fragments in all directions and filled the air with dust and the smell of gunpowder. The cannonballs and larger chunks of rock missed the three friends, but not by much.

As the pirate scrambled up the rigging to reload, Bobbie Bear asked Randolph, "Can you fly us out of this?"

Randolph shook his head no.

Bobbie Bear yelled out to Sam, "We have got to get off this ledge before we are blown to bits. Our only hope is to walk along that narrow path to the East cave. My legs are too short to make it, so you will have to carry me. Here, put this book back in your pocket. Get going!"

Sam felt so cold, wet, and terrified that he didn't

care what Randolph or Bobbie Bear thought of him, or if they left him forever.

"I want to go home!" Sam wailed. "I just wanted to have enough courage to play on the swings at recess! Now I'm being shot at and risking my life on a cliff!"

Bobbie Bear ignored Sam's plea and climbed onto his shoulders.

Sam forced himself to step onto the narrow, rain-slick path. In some places a thick growth of moss made the footing even more treacherous. A war raged inside Sam's head: *Don't think about falling. Oh, nuts, now I'm thinking about falling. Don't think about falling, don't think about falling! Oh man, now that's all I can think about. Think about reaching that East cave safely without falling. Now I'm thinking about falling again.*

As they made their way along the narrow path, the pirate fired the cannons again and again. One cannonball smashed into the cliff close to Sam, sending a rock fragment ripping through the sleeve of his jacket.

"Do not look down! Look up or straight ahead!" Bobbie shouted in Sam's ear. "Just pretend you are on a sidewalk."

Sam thought about making up a little poem or song to calm himself, but he just couldn't. Instead, he tried hard to imagine walking on a nice, safe sidewalk in the friendly neighborhood near his house.

In two minutes, which to Sam felt like two hours,

the three friends were at the mouth of the high-ceilinged east cave, where Randolph raised his leg against one wall. As Sam put Bobbie Bear down, she complimented him. "You did very well. That took real courage."

Sam felt proud of himself. He thought maybe the Grumpy Old Man had given him good advice after all.

A final salvo from the cannons barely missed them, with one cannonball whizzing inches from Sam's ear. Seeking safety, the three scampered deeper into the cave. There they found a very strange sight.

Chapter 12. Captain Pump

Sam noticed that the stream running through the cave hardly had the energy to move.

Inside, the cave had smooth gray walls and a poorly shaped wharf. Sam thought the cave and wharf looked slightly melted, as though no one had bothered to finish them. Stranger still, a sleek wooden ship about one hundred feet long with the name *Daisy* painted on the stern floated a few feet above the cave floor. The ship bobbed slightly in rhythm with the air currents passing through the cave. Curiously, Sam saw no masts or sails on the ship.

As he and his two friends drew closer to it, he asked Bobbie Bear, "Is that one of the ships that fly between the worlds?"

"Yes, she is. Notice her stern. Ships in your world have one rudder that moves left and right. That ship also has a second rudder that moves up and down. She is a small ship, but she looks fast, like a small version of the kind they call a clipper ship. I wonder where her masts and sails are?"

Next to the wharf squatted a small, crudely built stone house with no door in the entrance and no glass in the windows.

Sam yelled out, "Hello! Is anyone here?"

A man stumbled out of the house and blinked a few times. Sam saw that the man appeared round and soft, the way the inside of the cave looked. As the three approached, Sam also noticed what the man wore and what the pirate wore matched exactly, except that this man's shoes were scuffed, his clothes looked rumpled and worn, and his mustache hung limp. Sam wasn't sure what to make of this.

The man gazed at the visitors for a long time, bewildered. As the details slowly sunk in, his expression changed from confusion to surprise.

Normally Sam's fears included grown-ups he didn't know, but after his recent successes with the Grumpy Old Man, flying through the storm, and surviving the pirate, Sam felt much more confident. He marched up to the man and, using his best manners, said, "Hello, my name is Sam, this is Bobbie Bear, and the dog sniffing your pants is Randolph Coyote the Third."

The man hemmed and hawed, then finally responded. "Um, hello. I, uh, haven't had visitors for a very long time."

An awkward silence followed. Bobbie Bear finally asked, "And your name, sir?"

"Oh, um, Captain Pump. Captain of the *Daisy*."

"A very fine ship, sir," Bobbie Bear replied, trying to be pleasant.

They stood in silence waiting for Captain Pump's response. To Sam it seemed like they were waiting for some remote part of Captain Pump's brain to function after a long period of disuse. At last Captain Pump asked, "Would you care to come in and have some hot chocolate?"

"Yes, Randolph and I would love some, but none for Bobbie Bear, please," Sam answered as Bobbie Bear nodded in agreement.

As soon as Captain Pump ambled into the house, Randolph trotted over to a corner of the yard and raised his leg. Sam hissed at him, "We're guests here!"

"Hey, there's no harm in it. It's what I do," replied Randolph.

Sam shook his head in dismay. As Randolph trotted off to sniff around the cave, Sam and Bobbie Bear entered the house and sat on a stone bench built into the wall of the front room. Captain Pump came back shortly with three simple mugs, each of them cracked. Sam found the hot chocolate weak and not very warm but still refreshing after his harrowing experiences.

When he had finished his hot chocolate, Sam politely said, "Thank you so much. This was just what we needed." Hoping to learn more about Captain Pump's curious situation, he added, "The *Daisy* seems to be a very fine ship. Do you sail her often?"

"Um, no. Ah, I haven't been out of this cave in years."

"Years?" he asked. Despite Sam's eagerness to go home, he also wanted to find out what had kept Captain Pump in this dreary cave for so long.

"Yes. I've been exiled to this mountain, with this cave as my home, and I deserve it. I am so very guilty. I did very bad things out in the world, so my banishment to this place is perfectly fair." Captain Pump yawned and added sleepily, "I am nothing but a common criminal. I'd love to go out in the world and do good to make up for my misdeeds, but for now I think I'll just take a nap." With that, Captain Pump finished his hot chocolate and curled up on the stone bench along the opposite wall.

Captain Pump's statement baffled Sam. He wanted to ask more questions, but the captain began snoring almost immediately.

Bobbie Bear said, "That does not sound like the whole story."

Randolph ambled in, sniffed at Captain Pump, and drank his hot chocolate in two big slurps. "What's with him?" he inquired.

Sam shrugged and answered, "He needs a nap, I guess."

Bobbie Bear gathered up the empty cups and took them into the other room. There she found a simple kitchen and a worktable with a half-darned sock and a magnificent model ship on it. "Gentlemen, come look at this!" she said.

Randolph and Sam were impressed. The model, about two feet long, seemed to Sam to be a detailed replica of a clipper ship. Sam looked closely and saw that the sails and rigging of the model all seemed fully functional. He smiled with delight as he turned and pushed the tiny wheel gently and saw the rudders move. Captain Pump had painted *Daisy* on her stern. Sam realized that the ship at the wharf and the model looked exactly the same.

Sam suggested, "Captain Pump is still sleeping. Let's go outside and take a look at the real *Daisy*."

Sam and Bobbie Bear climbed aboard the clipper ship. Sam had lived his entire life near the ocean and knew sailboats quite well, but the cockpit of the *Daisy* looked different. Sam saw two large levers on either side of the wheel, and a steel shaft that went through the deck, all positioned so they would be easy for the helmsman to reach.

"What are these?" Sam asked Bobbie Bear as he grabbed one of the levers.

"Do not touch those!" Bobbie warned. Sam pulled his hand away. "Those are used to control the ship in flight."

Randolph padded very slowly along the wharf, carefully looking at the ship and sniffing the hull. When he finished his survey, Randolph explained to Sam and Bobbie Bear, "Look here, here, and here. The wood and paint in these areas do not match the rest of the hull. And these are small patches, no more than fifteen inches across, high up on her hull."

Sam guessed, "Maybe she banged into rocks?"

Randolph sniffed the wood and replied, "Maybe, but my guess is that these are repairs to the hull after cannon-balls hit her."

Bobbie Bear continued looking around, then called from the foredeck of the *Daisy,* "Gentlemen, come over here." When they got there, she pointed out that there were twenty gun carriages of the type used by muzzle-loading cannons, ten port, ten starboard, but no cannons. "Notice the twenty places where the deck railing has been cut away just enough to accommodate the barrel," said Bobbie Bear. "And look at the grooves in the deck behind the gun carriages. I think they were caused by the wheels of gun carriages when the guns were fired and recoiled, and when the guns were reloaded. It appears this ship has seen a lot of action."

Randolph sniffed at the deck and replied, "There's no smell of gunpowder. If this ship has been in a battle, it happened a very long time ago."

Sam commented, "Somehow I just can't see Captain Pump sailing this ship into a battle."

Bobbie Bear nodded. "Neither can I."

Randolph suddenly raised his head, looked at the

entrance to the cave, and pointed his ears in that direction, too. "Listen! The wind has died down!"

Bobbie Bear said, "Excellent. It is time for us to leave this place."

Suddenly an idea dawned on Randolph. He asked, "Hey, did you notice that the sails of the pirate who attacked us and the hull of the *Daisy* look like they would fit together perfectly? The holes in the deck of the *Daisy* match the size and shape of the pirate's masts. And both men look almost exactly alike, except one is lean and fierce, and the other round and soft."

"Yeah, you're right!" Sam said.

Randolph continued, "I'd really like to see what's in that other cave. I have a hunch that if we get the pirate and Captain Pump together we would do them and ourselves a lot of good. Besides, the Grumpy Old Man told Sam to solve the problem. Getting those two together might be the solution he talked about."

Randolph convinced Sam. "That's a good idea," Sam said.

But Randolph didn't convince Bobbie Bear at all. "If getting those two together is the solution, what is the problem?" she asked. "Captain Pump lives in one cave, and the pirate lives in the other cave. What is the problem with that?"

Sam now found himself swayed to Bobbie Bear's point of view. He nodded in agreement with her.

Bobbie Bear continued, "The wind has died down, and Randolph is rested and fit, so we are now able to leave. We have almost been killed several times. We should declare victory and go home."

Sam nodded even more vigorously and said, "Guys, I have something to admit to you. I went to the Grumpy Old Man because the playground equipment at school scared me to death. So did the school bus, grown-ups, and almost everything. You heard the Grumpy Old Man tell me to come here and solve the problem. Well, since we left my bedroom I have ridden on Randolph through two flashes, almost become lunch for a pterodactyl, got the information I needed from the Grumpy Old Man, flown through another flash and a storm, and carried Bobbie Bear along a sheer cliff on a narrow path while being shot at by a weird pirate. If I could do all that, I think the problem of me being scared of the swings at school is solved. Let's go home."

Bobbie Bear said, "That is very smart of you, Sam. I totally agree."

"Besides," Sam continued, "I feel like we've been gone for hours. If my parents wake up and I'm gone they'll freak."

Bobbie Bear answered, "That is probably not a problem. Time runs at different speeds in different flashes. In your world we have been gone . . ." Bobbie Bear studied her chronometer, turned one of its dials, and said, "Six minutes and fifteen seconds."

Randolph sighed, "Are you sure you want to go home?"

"Yes!" Bobbie Bear and Sam said at the same time.

Bobbie Bear reset her navigation instruments. She dialed some numbers on her brass course calculator to be ready to search for Sam's part of the Rainbow Flash, or at least a flash that would lead them to it. They all put on their goggles, and Sam settled on Randolph's back with Bobbie Bear in front of him. The three skimmed over the floor of the east cave and out. But instead of flying up to where a flash might be, Randolph's curiosity about the other cave got the better of him. He made a hard U-turn and headed for the West cave.

"No, no! Turn around!" yelled Sam and Bobbie Bear as they both yanked on his harness, but Randolph flew into the West cave anyway.

They entered the cave to find the pirate's guns pointed directly at them. The pirate himself sat in a velvet chair on the wharf, sipping from a china cup. In his left hand he held a line that controlled the cannons' fuses.

He gave the three friends an evil smile and said sweetly, "I've been expecting you."

Chapter 13. Captain Kin

The pirate waved a lace handkerchief toward the guns and answered, “Have a seat or I’ll blow your heads off. Please, make yourselves comfortable.” He waved the handkerchief toward a gaudy couch and matching coffee table.

Sam and Bobbie Bear shot Randolph a dirty look, as if to say, “See all the trouble you’ve gotten us into!”

The three friends realized they didn’t have much choice, so they sat on the couch, but on the edge, ready to run. Sam looked around at the huge, complex cave made of sharp-edged stones that were either very dark or very light. A stream bounded through the cave with untamed energy, and many passageways led off from the main chamber. A grand palace near the cave’s wharf dominated the cavern. The palace’s walls of finely crafted marble gave off a soft glow that contrasted with the gleam of its golden rooftops. A grand staircase led to tall oak doors. The many windows of stained glass and the tall towers sporting brightly colored silk pendants added a feeling of gaiety that Sam found odd in such a dangerous situation.

Sam looked up at the threat facing them and counted the guns tied to the spars. There were twenty. He remembered that there were twenty gun carriages on the *Daisy*. This baffled him.

"Please forgive my rudeness," the pirate said with great formality and a wave of his handkerchief. "The name I go by is Captain Kin, the most feared pirate in all the worlds. And you are?"

"Randolph Coyote the Third, Bobbie Bear, and I'm Sam."

"I am very pleased to have you as my guests. I've never had any visitors."

"I am not surprised. You tried to kill us!" Bobbie Bear exclaimed.

Captain Kin dealt with the objection with a wave of his lace handkerchief. "Oh, that. I thought you had been sent by my archenemy. Tell me, why are you here?"

"The Grumpy Old Man sent us," Sam answered.

"Never heard of him. Why did he send you here?"

"Well, I lacked courage because my imagination kept getting in the way of my doing stuff other kids do, so he sent me here."

"Did it work?" asked Captain Kin with great interest as he leaned forward in his chair.

"I think so," Sam answered.

"Yes, it did," Bobbie Bear confirmed. "I think Sam is very courageous."

Sam almost blushed. "Thanks, Bobbie Bear."

"I agree," added Captain Kin. "Well done, lad."

Sam beamed with pleasure, despite his fear of Captain Kin.

"Now, how many of you would care for some hot chocolate?" Captain Kin offered. "Two? Excellent! I'll be right back."

No sooner had Captain Kin entered his palace than Randolph began sniffing at Captain Kin's chair. Randolph looked puzzled and commented, "This is very odd. Captain Pump and Captain Kin smell nearly the same. I've never run into two people whose smells were so close."

Randolph sniffed around more, bounded over to the bottom step of the palace entrance, and raised his leg just as Captain Kin came out.

"Ah well, dogs will be dogs," Captain Kin said amiably. He carried a silver tray with three fine china cups on saucers, which he set on the coffee table.

"Mmm," Sam said. "This is the best hot chocolate I've ever tasted!"

Captain Kin seemed genuinely pleased. "A boy with courage and good taste. I'm getting to like you, lad. Maybe I won't blow your head off. I'll save my cannon-balls for that oaf Captain Pump, if he ever stops working on that model ship and comes out of that hovel he lives in."

"You seem to know a lot about Captain Pump," remarked Randolph as he returned from his sniffing expedition. He hopped up on the couch and lapped at his hot chocolate.

"I should. I was him, or at least half of him. In order to understand what happened to me allow me to tell you what happened to my ancestor, Roscoe, many, many years ago, long before I was born."

Chapter 14. Roscoe's Story

"Roscoe grew up poor. Stomach-growling, rag-wearing, roof-leaking, barefoot-in-winter poor. But while the eight children in his family often went to bed with empty bellies, they never went to bed without a story. His father worked as a poorly paid blacksmith for Lord Bernard, but, despite his exhaustion, he never missed story-time. The stories were often the same, a boy both brave and smart was heir to the throne, but was cheated out of his inheritance by an evil relative. The boy grows up poor but becomes a great warrior who returns home, kills the evil relation, and claims the throne. Perhaps a bit trite, but they loved that story. His father would vary the details, but the plots were always about the same. Roscoe listened to that story every night as the population of the children's bed diminished, girls leaving for marriage, boys leaving to fight in the endless wars. Soon it was just Roscoe, the youngest, in the bed, still too young to leave.

"Now I must tell you something peculiar about the kingdom Roscoe grew up in. In most kingdoms, when the king dies the old king's eldest son becomes the new king. But in that kingdom the old king named his successor before he died, and he could name anyone. It could be the youngest son, or a distant cousin. The reading of the king's will and the naming of his successor was usually done in an elaborate ceremony with the entire court present.

"The old king was named Sebastian, a man more interested in raucous parties than attending to the business of the kingdom.

"When Roscoe was five Sebastian, the old king, died without writing his will or carrying out the ceremony naming a successor. What everyone feared would happen did happen. Civil war broke out, with a number of nobles claiming the throne. The original claimants were quickly murdered by other claimants, who were also quickly murdered by yet other would-be successors.

"Documents appeared claiming to be the authentic will of Sebastian, the old king. All were forgeries. And this is where my story becomes less than credible, but is true. Every word. By the way, would either of you like some more hot cocoa?"

"No, no!" Sam cried out. "What happened?! Tell us what happened!"

Captain Kin smiled and continued.

"The murder and mayhem continued until one winner began to emerge out of the chaos, Reginald, the most violent and ruthless of all the contenders, a man who enjoyed all the killing.

"One of the last would-be successors for Reginald to eliminate was Lord Bernard, who found out that Reginald planned to kill him. To gain enough time to escape, Bernard needed a diversion. He ordered Cyril the scribe, one of his vassals, to write a document that looked like the last will and testament of Sebastian. To muddy the waters as much as possible, the document named the most obscure of Bernard's servants, his blacksmith's little boy, five-year-old Roscoe, as the next king, proving, I suppose, that, if nothing else, Bernard had a sense of humor.

When the murderous Reginald got a copy of the bogus will, he was torn. Who should he have murdered first, Bernard or Roscoe? Reginald didn't know anything about either of them, but he once had a horse named Roscoe whom he disliked, so he sent his henchmen off to murder Roscoe and all related to him.

"On his way to escape Bernard gave a copy of the bogus will to his blacksmith, Roscoe's father, in the hope that his blacksmith would flee and thus be more time-consuming to find.

Roscoe's father read the document, realized the implications, packed up his wife and son and his few possessions, and fled.

"Roscoe's mother had a brother who was captain of a long-haul freighter, so they went to the nearest port. They asked around and picked up a rumor that the brother might have been at a port far away. They spent the next year chasing him, Roscoe's father working as a blacksmith to earn passage at each step. Finally, they connected with him, and the brother agreed to take on Roscoe as an apprentice sailor.

"And that is how my family got involved with ships. Oddly enough, Roscoe's mother, my great great great grandmother Ruth, never got rid of that bogus will, so all through his life there was always the hint of a rumor that Roscoe was of noble birth, a rumor Roscoe found useful to cultivate.

"If all this happened long ago how do you know so much?" Sam asked.

"Ah, good question! Smart lad. Bernard felt that he was genius, and that every word he spoke should be preserved. Do you remember Cyril the scribe? He had Cyril follow him around and write his every utterance. Some of those parchments survived, and, from them, I was able to piece together a history of what happened.

"Now it is time to talk about my favorite subject, me."

Chapter 15. Captain Kin's Story

"I was born to a family of substantial means. My father was the greatest of the Master Navigators. He was paid extremely well to guide ships through passages that were impassable to lessor men, but he was seldom home. I barely remember him. When I was fifteen he used his considerable influence to get me a position as a midshipman aboard the Blue-Green-Yellow, the greatest warship of her day. Of course, he secured positions for my brothers as well, but mine was the most significant.

"I served in the Navy for years, all through the wars. Toward the end of the Blue-Green wars I was assigned to privateer duty. After the war, with no work available, I drifted into piracy.

"I became the most successful pirate ever. Whole worlds trembled at the mention of my name. I plundered merchants and became rich, but only in comparison to other pirates. I never forgot my connection to nobility.

"One day I was sitting alone in the little garden of a tavern, enjoying the warm sunshine, when four noisy young noblemen came in. They saw that I was well dressed and began mocking me, saying that no matter how much money I had I would always be a commoner. Of course, I was rumored to be heir to a throne, but of a kingdom far away that I had never seen. Despite being boiling mad, and wanting nothing more than to put those puppies in their place, I held my tongue and walked back to my ship.

"The entire incident with the noblemen took less than a minute, but it changed my life. I resolved to conquer my ancestral kingdom, but to do that I needed to raise an army, which is hugely expensive. I was rich, but not that rich. I brooded over the problem.

"A year after my encounter with the noble puppies, an ordinary looking businessman came to my island of treasure. He offered to make me so wealthy I would be able to raise ten armies. Despite his humdrum appearance, that man struck fear in every heart, for he practiced the dark arts more powerfully than anyone else. Whole worlds trembled at his very name, the mighty sorcerer Mr. Bland!"

"Mr. Bland? That doesn't sound very scary," Sam commented.

Captain Kin leaned forward and said seriously, "A word to the wise, my friend. Never underestimate Mr. Bland. He would strike you dead at the merest smirk. So, on with my story.

"Mr. Bland's appearance might have made him

seem ordinary, but his powers were terrifying. He and I signed a contract stating that Mr. Bland would guide me to rich prey. In return, I agreed to give ten percent of my take to Mr. Bland and never attack any of the merchant ships he owned. This arrangement worked well for years. At first, I possessed enough gold to hire a hundred soldiers, then enough to hire a thousand, and then ten thousand. Mr. Bland, a mere commoner, grew mad with jealousy when he saw me drawing ever closer to my royal goal.

"Finally, Mr. Bland's jealousy became too much for him to bear. He could stand it no more. Some scallywag plundered one of his ships. I told him I was innocent, but that meant nothing to Mr. Bland. He accused me and carried out his awful punishment.

"A storm cloud appeared over my ship, and Mr. Bland swooped down. I fired my guns at him, but all the cannonballs missed. Bland banished my crew to land and split Captain Pumpkin in half. One half became Captain Pump, that lazy, pudgy recluse who blames himself for everything and wants to do good but never gets around to it. The other half became me, Captain Kin, your host, with all the energy, wit, and charm. Mr. Bland also divided the ship. Pump got the hull, I got the sails, spars, and guns. He banished us to this miserable mountain for two hundred years. It has been more than two hundred years, but that hardly matters. Despite my innocence, I'll be stuck here forever."

Captain Kin looked closely at his guests to see if they believed his tale.

"That's terrible!" Sam cried out. "That's the saddest story I've ever heard! What happened to you is so unfair!"

"Yes, lad, it certainly is! But what's to be done? Pump and I both want to get off this mountain, but every time I approach Pump he flees in terror. Alone, neither one of us have the ability to leave. It would take both of us working together. Pump wants to make beautiful model ships, but he doesn't have the energy to accomplish anything. He has completed only one model ship in two hundred years. I, on the other hand, am full of energy and ambition, but I can't do very much without the hull. Ah, the great things I could do! The worlds I could conquer! But really, if we try to leave this mountain, Mr. Bland would know about it in a moment and make our lives even more miserable."

Bobbie Bear asked Captain Kin, "Did you read the contract before you signed it?"

"I tried, but it was so boring I couldn't get past the first page."

"When did you last see Mr. Bland?" Sam asked.

"Many, many years ago. Perhaps he's dead or has gone off to do other things."

Bobbie Bear asked, "Do you have a copy of the contract you and Mr. Bland signed?"

"Why, yes, I do! It's at the bottom of my trunk."

Bobbie Bear explained, "It might state that you are free to go at the end of two hundred years. If you do not mind, could Randolph and I read it?"

"Oh, yes, I would appreciate that. After all, I am without proper clerical help. I'll try to find it. Give me a minute or two to dig it out."

After Captain Kin entered his palace, Randolph Coyote the Third commented to Sam, "What hooey! That business about his connection to royalty and escaping assassins sounds like a half-baked fairy tale."

"Really?" Sam said, shocked. "But if it isn't true, why would he say it?"

Bobbie Bear shrugged and commented, "I do not know why. However, parts of his story may be true. Based on what we have seen of Captains Pump and Kin, and how the *Daisy* and her spars would fit together, it is entirely possible that someone split Captain Pumpkin in half and exiled him here. Making Captain Pumpkin whole again might solve the problem mentioned by the Grumpy Old Man. It sounds like a worthwhile thing to do."

Randolph nodded and said, "Yes, it certainly does. Now aren't you glad I brought you to this cave?"

Both Bobbie Bear and Sam said at the same time, "No!"

Captain Kin came out of his house with the contract, which he dropped with a thud on the coffee table.

Sam had never seen a contract before. He turned a

few pages out of curiosity. He couldn't make sense of the tiny, though very neat, lettering. "Is this what all contracts are like?" Sam asked Bobbie Bear.

"No, not at all," she replied. "A contract is really just an agreement between people. Some are not written at all. Two people might make a business agreement verbally, and that can be a contract. This one is much longer than usual and is written by hand on parchment, which was a common practice long ago."

Bobbie Bear and Randolph Coyote the Third began reading the document. The fact that neither showed any concern about its size impressed Sam. They pointed out sections to each other, chuckling as they flew through it.

Sam looked over their shoulders and tried to make sense of it but couldn't. "How come you guys are laughing?" he asked them.

Randolph answered, "Oh, this contract looks pretty impressive at first glance, but if you know what to look for you can see that it's a real stinker. There are a lot of contradictions. It says one thing here, then a few pages later it says the complete opposite. For example, Section 13, Paragraph 2 contradicts Section 13, Paragraph 1."

In what seemed like no time at all Randolph and Bobbie Bear finished. "Well, this contract is truly a mess," Bobbie Bear reported. "But, on the whole, it looks like you can leave."

"Wonderful!" Captain Kin exclaimed. "Let's get going."

"What needs to happen, and how can we help?" Bobbie Bear asked.

Captain Kin answered, "When the *Daisy* is put back together, my guess is that Pump and I will be, too. So, all you have to do is get Pump's cooperation, or at least have the *Daisy* where I can get to it."

Bobbie Bear explained, "We will fly to the East cave and see what we can do."

But when they got to the East cave, the three friends cried out in dismay. Captain Pump and his ship were gone.

Chapter 16. Getting It Together

Randolph Coyote the Third rallied his friends. "Goggles on! Let's go find Captain Pump and his ship."

They flew out of the cave and into bright sunshine. The retreating storm had left behind crisp air and gusty winds that sent fat cumulus clouds scudding across the sky. For the first time, Sam enjoyed riding Randolph, as they soared over granite ridges and swooped down through valleys filled with colorful wildflowers. But though they searched everywhere, they could not find the *Daisy*. They landed in a field of flowers and stretched out in the warm sunshine.

As he started drifting off to sleep, Sam casually mentioned, "If the *Daisy* doesn't have sails I wonder how Captain Pump got her out of the cave."

"That ship can move a little without sails, but not well and not far," Bobbie Bear replied.

Randolph sat up, his ears alert. "Did you say not far?"

"Yes, not far."

"She is probably close to the cave. Wake up, lazy bones!" Randolph ordered Sam as he gave him a powerful nudge with his snout. "I know how to find the *Daisy*."

They flew back to the ledge where they had first landed on Thunder Mountain, a place that had seemed so scary. Now he enjoyed the spectacular view of the cliffs on the other side of the valley.

Randolph advised, "Stay on board. We're gonna have to move fast."

Randolph filled his lungs and let out a howl so powerful, so bloodcurdling it made the hair on Sam's neck stand up. Randolph flew straight up very fast as the howl echoed from cliff to cliff, sounding like dozens of creatures straight out of a nightmare.

As the three friends scanned the rugged landscape below, Sam saw the bow of the *Daisy* poke out from under an overhang and then disappear again. It looked to him like Captain Pump had moved the ship from its hiding place in the narrow canyon when he heard Randolph's howl, but then changed his mind.

"There!" Sam pointed, and Randolph plunged toward the outcrop with stomach wrenching speed, making Sam shriek with terror.

As soon as they were on the *Daisy*'s deck, Sam complained to Randolph, "You didn't need to dive like that."

Randolph just chuckled.

Sam composed himself and turned to Captain

Pump. In his friendliest voice, he said, "Captain Pump, we have a superb plan."

Captain Pump whined, "I know all about your plan because Kin and I are really one person. I'm scared and tired—all I want to do is take a nap. You'll only make things worse. Go away."

"Do you want to stay here forever?" asked Randolph.

"Well, I have gotten used to it. It's not too bad, really."

For the first time in his life, Sam took charge of the situation. He said to Randolph, "Leave Bobbie Bear and me here, find Captain Kin, and bring him to us with his sails and masts."

As soon as Randolph left, Bobbie Bear asked Captain Pump, "Would you be kind enough to move the *Daisy* out from under this overhang?"

Captain Pump gave no answer. Instead he moved away from them as far as he could and sat on the deck with his back to them.

Bobbie Bear said, "It looks like we will have to move the ship ourselves. If we do not move her out from under this overhang, we will not be able to step the masts. Before we move the ship, we need to put out fenders along the port side. Fenders are those things made of rope that protect the sides of the ship if we bump into something, like the wall of this canyon."

When they were finished swinging fenders over the

side of the ship, Bobbie Bear said, "Excellent. Now, you will notice that the ship is under this overhang with her starboard side against the canyon wall. We need to move her so she is out in the open with her port side against the other wall of the canyon. Get me that boathook over there and I will show you how to move a ship sideways about two hundred feet."

Bobbie Bear stood in the center of the ship on the starboard side and set the boathook against the rock cliff. She asked Sam, "Help me push against the cliff with the boathook."

"Just the two of us are going to move the big ship? No way!"

"This is an excellent ship. It takes very little effort to move her," Bobbie Bear answered.

Sam shrugged. He grabbed the end of the boathook and pushed as hard as he could. The ship moved to port quite easily, which surprised Sam. As it glided across the narrow canyon, Bobbie Bear and Sam walked over the deck and stood with the boathook sticking out the port side. They pushed against the opposite wall as they approached, slowing the ship so she gently touched the rock wall.

"And that is how it is done," Bobbie Bear said.

Bobbie Bear went below decks, found an oilcan, and gave the wheel, steering gear, and flight controls, a generous oiling.

A few minutes later, Randolph returned sitting in the crow's nest next to Captain Kin. The pirate maneuvered the sails and spars directly over the *Daisy* and boomed, "This is more like it! We've got some action here! In no time, I'll conquer two or three worlds and raise an army and get back on the throne where I belong!"

Sam scratched his head and yelled back, "I thought you said your claim to the throne was bogus, that it was merely a part of Bernard's plan to escape."

Captain Kin twirled his mustache and said, "Ah, smart lad. You are correct! It would seem that way, but there might be more truth to that will than even I imagine. Sam, how would you like to be my viceroy for one of the worlds I'll conquer? You could rule an entire world!"

"No thank you. Being viceroy wouldn't leave me enough time to do my homework."

Bobbie Bear laughed so hard she fell over. Randolph jumped out of the crow's nest while laughing and almost crashed on the deck.

Captain Pump sat in the cockpit, curled up like a ball, totally confused.

Kin stood on the deck and focused on the masts. He expertly guided them until they were directly over the *Daisy,* and then lowered them until they fit securely in their steps, which held them to the bottom of the hull.

As soon as the masts were in place Kin marched over to Pump, shook him, and said, "Get up, Pump! Time to get together!"

"No, I don't want to. I'm scared, and I want to take a nap."

Sam asked, "What happens if he stays seated like that?"

"Nothing, and that's the problem," Kin replied. "We both have to be standing to make the getting together work."

Kin grabbed Pump by the belt and tried to force him up, but couldn't. Sam realized that both men were exactly equal in strength. Sam turned to Randolph and Bobbie Bear and asked, "Any ideas?"

Randolph said to Kin, "Let's both grab him by the belt and lift."

They did, and managed to get Pump a foot off the deck, but he was still curled up tight.

"Oh, I've got an idea," Sam said. "Lift Pump as high as you can get him and I'll try it."

As soon as Kin and Randolph got Pump as high as they could Sam tickled Pump under the chin.

Pump was so surprised that he giggled and straightened out.

Kin pulled hard.

Pump and Kin snapped together and, for the first time in 200 years, Captain Pumpkin emerged.

"This is better!" Captain Pumpkin roared. "Now, two quick stops and, young Sam, let's get you back home!"

They all cheered wildly at their success.

"Thank you, all three of you. It's a long time since I've been whole, and I can't tell you how great it feels," said the captain.

"You're welcome," Sam replied, blushing a little.

"Though I must tell you," Captain Pumpkin said, "That, should the need arise, I believe I could get myself back together again on my own, though that need will never arise. Well, now, Sam, we need to sort out the lines. Care to help?"

"Yes, sir!"

With Sam at his side, Captain Pumpkin strode the deck looking up at the sails flapping lazily in the breeze. Together they sorted out which sheet led to which sail and set the sheets, but very loosely. The sails continued their lazy flapping.

Looking up, Sam noticed something odd. "What are those little gizmos on either side of the top of each mast?" he asked.

"They hold pixie pollen so we can shrink the entire ship and crew down to fit through a flash and then, on the other side, regain our normal size."

"Cool," said Sam.

They went back to the cockpit. The captain grasped the shaft that went through the deck, twisted the handle a quarter turn, and pulled it up about an inch until it clicked once. Sam couldn't feel any change in the wind, but the sails filled with a snap and the timbers of the hull groaned as the *Daisy* rose very slowly, shaking off two hundred years of idleness. When the *Daisy* gained enough altitude to clear the canyon walls, Captain Pumpkin pushed the starboard lever forward slightly. The ship's bow began to swing slowly to port. Sam grabbed a railing, convinced the groaning was the sound of the *Daisy* coming apart, but the sound didn't faze Captain Pumpkin a bit. The captain kept one hand on the wheel, the other on the starboard lever, and his eyes constantly scanning the sails and the rocky terrain.

The *Daisy* slowly moved forward with the power of a wind Sam couldn't sense at all, but nothing could hide the thrill Sam felt as the ship came to life.

Captain Pumpkin expertly sailed around the rocks and slipped into what had been Captain Kin's cave, where he tied up at the dock.

Warm sunshine poured onto the mouth of the cave. Bobbie Bear sat in the entrance and took out the quartz crystals from a pouch in her belly. She lay them in the sun and seemed to sleep.

Captain Pumpkin went to the *Daisy*'s galley and discovered a barrel of dried, salted beef. Both he and Randolph sniffed at the contents and, to their surprise, found the meat was still good. Randolph wolfed down thirty pounds of it. Afterward he drank from the stream, curled up in the cockpit, and began snoring.

Captain Pumpkin asked Sam for help, and the two of them went into Captain Kin's house.

They returned pulling a crude wooden cart containing a large, heavy, wooden box. They struggled to carry it below decks on the *Daisy*. At last they managed to slip it into a receptacle that kept it secure in the cabin and within sight of the helmsman.

Captain Pumpkin opened the steel lock and lifted the lid, revealing a collection of gold-plated navigational instruments.

"Wow!" Sam said,

Beautifully crafted navigational instruments seemed to glow softly against the black velvet of the inside of the case.

A three-dimensional sextant, one much bigger and more complex than Bobbie Bear's, occupied the middle of the case. Sam looked closely and saw that it had its own windup clock mechanism. Five compasses occupied the space to the left of the sextant, and to the right sat two chronometers, one running clockwise, and the other counterclockwise.

"We have much work to do now, lad. Later I will show you how some of this navigation gear works," Captain Pumpkin said as he carefully closed the lid.

Pumpkin went below decks and came back up a few minutes later barefoot and dressed in simple work clothes.

"Clothes make the man," Captain Pumpkin said to

Sam, "And clothes wrecked from hard work leave a poor impression. So now, let's get to work."

Sam and Captain Pumpkin worked hard to transport items from Captain Kin's house to the ship. They moved cannonballs, gunpowder, barrels for fresh water, boxes of salted meat, and an enormously heavy box containing almanacs. Randolph flew as many loads as he could to the ship. He also helped pull the wooden cart.

They made many trips back and forth and stowed everything securely on board the *Daisy*.

While they worked, Bobbie Bear, still sitting in the sunshine at the cave entrance, woke up. She tucked the recharged crystals back in her pouch, strolled to the *Daisy*, and sat in the cockpit thumbing through formulas at the back of one of the almanacs.

When at last Sam, Randolph, and Captain Pumpkin finished, they joined her in the cockpit and rested.

"How did you learn to handle a ship so well?" Sam asked Captain Pumpkin.

Hearing these words, Randolph lay down in a comfortable spot and rotated his ears toward Captain Pumpkin. Bobbie Bear and Sam also found relaxing places to sit as he told his story.

Chapter 17. Captain Pumpkin

Captain Pumpkin laughed. "How I learned ship handling? Oh, that's a tale," he said as he ducked below decks, grabbed his shoes, good clothes, and a box of supplies. As he spoke he meticulously polished his shoes and all the brass buckles and buttons, and mended his garments.

"I'll tell you, lad, there's nothing that impresses the ladies like a man who dresses sharp, dances lively, and has some gold jingling in his pocket. Now then, as for my tale.

"My family was poor. Sometimes, around the fire at night, my parents would talk about the wealth my family had ages ago, before the accident. When he worked, my father made good money, but a shipboard accident left him crippled. When the pain wasn't too bad he made a poor living teaching navigation. The money my parents had saved vanished long before I came along. My ma and pa had eight children, seven boys and the youngest a girl. I was the seventh. Only three of my brothers lived past childhood, and all three went off on the ships and died on voyages. When I was ten-years-old war broke out. The Royal Navy desperately needed anyone who could pull a rope. I signed up. My parents' lives were so hard that they could spare little energy for caring. They wished me luck and sighed with relief to have one less mouth to feed.

"Life on warships suited me, and I rose in the ranks. At age twenty, I earned my first command. At twenty-two, I commanded a larger ship. By age twenty-three a group of businessmen asked me to be captain of a privateer they planned to finance. At that time, my government allowed privately owned warships to attack and seize the cargo of ships from an enemy country. The rules for privateers during that war were very strict. Only the cargo could be seized, and only from an enemy ship. My crew, our backers, and I were to be paid a percentage of the cargo we captured, with the rest going to our government."

"That sounds a lot like piracy," Randolph commented.

"Very close. Back then, when one government wanted to inflict damage on another, they could license privateers, which would save the Crown the expense of paying for a navy. Some successful privateers made a lot of money, but for us things went badly. We roamed all the known worlds, but every ship we encountered either flew a friendly flag or carried so many guns that we dared not attack. Finally, we ran out of food and money. We limped back to home port poor, skinny, and dressed in rags. The fury of the businessmen who had backed us hit us like a storm. We had failed, and they lost everything they had put into the venture.

"To make matters worse, the war ended. The ports filled with ex-officers looking for any job they could get. The navy didn't want us, and there would be no more businessmen backing privateers.

"Then I survived the hardest year of my life. I eked out a miserable existence as a stevedore, breaking my back lifting cargo in and out of ships. I earned barely enough to buy morsels of spoiling food. After a year, I could take no more. My body was in ruins, and my spirit demolished. I found the darkest corner of that vile port, lay down, and fell into a deep, dreamless sleep.

"But then the strangest thing happened. I awoke, opened my eyes, and saw the polished shoes of a well-dressed man. I thought I had died, but I hadn't. I looked up and saw Mr. Bland for the first time.

"Mr. Bland hired people to nurse me back to health, and then he made me a most interesting offer. He said he would finance a pirate ship and make me captain. Privateers were pirates backed by governments, and if captured they were treated as prisoners of war. However, Mr. Bland proposed real piracy. If we were caught we would all be hanged. I had reached such depths of despair that I decided I had nothing to lose. An important part of the contract stated that I could never attack a ship flying Mr. Bland's company flag. At the time, that seemed a minor point. Besides, Bland offered a tempting bonus. If I brought in a certain amount of loot within one year, the ship would be mine. I would be transformed from a starving harbor rat to the owner of a ship. What a turn of fortune! I signed the contract on the spot.

"Mr. Bland told me the best locations and times to find rich merchantmen, and we robbed them without mercy. Bland seemed to have a genius for finding pixie pollen—the richest cargo anyone could hope for. I pushed my men as hard as I could, but they didn't mind, since their pay was a percentage of the take, and they were growing rich. As captain, I got an even larger percentage and my wealth grew and grew. After three hundred and sixty-four days, I had stolen almost enough to get the ship, but not quite, when I spotted a rich merchant's ship, but it flew the Bland flag. My lust to be a ship's owner blinded me to danger. My officers begged me to sail around the ship, but I gave the order to attack!

"That Bland ship carried the richest plunder any of us had ever seen. The ship groaned under the weight of thousands of casks of pixie pollen. We worked feverishly to move as much of the cargo onto our ship as she would hold. After we had taken our fill we sent the Bland ship on her way. Naturally I wouldn't get a bonus from Bland, nor would he give me the ship, but with this rich cargo in my hold I didn't care. My crew and I were suddenly struck by the fact that we had all just become very, very wealthy.

"We set course for a port where we knew they wouldn't ask how we came by our rich cargo. We were well on our way when our nightmare began.

"Mr. Bland swooped down from a dark cloud in the sky and headed for our ship. With terror in their eyes, my crew looked over their shoulders as they frantically pulled on the lines to wring every possible bit of speed out of this very ship that we sit in now, the *Daisy*. The wooden hull and masts groaned under the strain. The sails nearly burst as the ship shot forward. When the *Daisy* had gained as much speed as I thought she could stand, I swung the wheel hard. The ship heeled over, raising the guns to bear on our foe. The guns boomed, and cannonballs flew directly at Mr. Bland, but they did no damage. Mr. Bland flew around them easily and landed on our ship.

"The wind that blows between the worlds instantly went out of the *Daisy's* sails, and she stopped dead. Bland calmly walked to the cargo hold and peered in. He surveyed the evidence of our plunder and reached inside his silk jacket for his quill pen. With one wave of that pen he banished my crew to land. With another he split me in half and sentenced me to two hundred years on Thunder Mountain. Kin told you the rest, and here I am today."

While Captain Pumpkin told his tale, Sam sat very still, committing every detail of the story to memory.

"Now then, Sam, that's enough of my yarn. We need

to get those guns out of the rigging and down onto their carriages. Come give me a hand," Captain Pumpkin urged.

Sam shook himself out of his reverie and said, "Yes, sir!"

As they started to work, Sam asked, "How much does each gun weigh?"

"About as much as a large, fully grown man," Captain Pumpkin answered. "They are too heavy to just tuck under your arm and carry, so we'll use block and tackle for the job. I'll go up the ratlines, you stay on deck and ease each gun down with the block and tackle. By the time you get it down, I'll be on deck to help you push the gun into its carriage."

In short order, the guns were out of the rigging and secured in their carriages. The hard work of moving supplies onto the *Daisy* and lowering the guns out of the rigging did not faze Captain Pumpkin, who had the strength of a man who'd spent years working on sailing ships, but it exhausted young Sam. Although Sam tried to hide his fatigue, the captain saw he needed rest and said, "I'm feeling a bit tired. Let's take a break."

Sam sat in the cockpit sipping water while Captain Pumpkin opened the navigation box and wound up the chronometer.

"That is very beautiful equipment," exclaimed Bobbie Bear, opening her pouch to show Captain Pumpkin her own navigation devices.

"Very nice," he said. "Simple but effective, and much easier to transport than all of this."

"Yes, but yours will get you to the exact location you want without any guesswork and use a minimum of pixie pollen," Bobbie Bear replied.

"True, there are advantages to both." Turning to Sam, Captain Pumpkin added, "Come on, lad, there's more work to be done."

"Yes, sir!" Sam replied, ready to get back to work after his rest. Sam wanted to see the ship and the navigation equipment in operation.

Bobbie Bear called out, "Wait! Something just occurred to me. We do not want to unleash something bad. We will help you, Captain, if you promise to give up piracy."

"I've been thinking about doing that for many years," Captain Pumpkin admitted. "After all I've been through that's exactly what I intend to do." He stood next to the wheel, held up his right hand, and solemnly swore, "I promise to give up piracy."

The three friends applauded Captain Pumpkin. The captain bowed deeply. Then he turned to his navigation equipment. After he had finished setting it to their new location, he asked Sam, "When you came here, did you see a flash of light?"

Sam looked at Randolph, wondering if he should tell Captain Pumpkin that he came from the Blue-Green-Yellow Flash, or if he should tell the truth.

Randolph said to Captain Pumpkin, "Sam comes from way out in the Rainbow Flash."

"Ah, the Rainbow Flash. That's a long way. Never visited any of those worlds, and don't know anyone who has, but that tells me a bit of what I need to know to set our course," he said. "Bobbie Bear, would you please use my navigation equipment to set an exact course to Sam's world."

While Bobbie Bear worked with the instruments Captain Pumpkin ducked below decks, quickly took off his work clothes, and donned his now gleaming and immaculate clothes.

"I guess we can't go back the way we came," Sam added.

Captain Pumpkin, looking over Bobbie Bear's shoulder, explained, "That's right. When you came here, you went from one world to another through at least one flash, and probably more. The flashes are in constant motion, always appearing and disappearing, but in fairly predictable ways. It's that predictability that makes navigation possible. With these instruments and books, I can generally get a ship to a desired location. Mine may not be the best route or the easiest, but I can usually get there without too much trouble. My navigation skills are adequate, but I have a feeling that Bobbie Bear's skills are better than mine. I never studied with gnomes."

Bobbie Bear thumbed through an almanac until she

found the right numbers. She carefully copied them onto a piece of paper. Next, she looked in the back of the book for the formulas she needed. She wrote them on another piece of paper and continued to calculate the course of navigation.

Without looking up, Bobbie Bear asked Sam, "How good is your math?"

"Not so good," Sam admitted.

Captain Pumpkin looked at him disapprovingly. "No excuse for that, young man. If you can't do math, you can't navigate. If you can't navigate, you're stuck where you are—marooned. Learn math." Sam nodded in agreement.

Bobbie Bear finished her calculations.

Captain Pumpkin said, "Just one more stop and we're on our way." He maneuvered the ship out of the West cave and into the East cave, where they tied up at the wharf.

He ran into the house. A few minutes later he came back carrying the model ship Captain Pump had taken two hundred years to build. He handed it to Sam. "Here, lad, a little gift for your help. Thanks to you and your friends I will finally be able to leave this place."

"Thank you, thank you, thank you!" Sam replied, beaming with pleasure.

"Just one more thing to do," announced Captain Pumpkin. He climbed up each mast to check the supplies of white and black pixie pollen. Sam noticed that he got to the top of each mast as easily as Sam could walk across a room.

"Thank goodness we've got plenty of pollen!" Captain Pumpkin reported. Then he cast off the dock lines and worked the levers, shaft, and wheel. They slipped out of the cave and into the dazzling sunshine and clear blue skies of a glorious day, all of them thinking that their troubles were over.

Chapter 18. The Terrifying Mr. Bland

Captain Pumpkin set their course as they flew, and they quickly reached the right altitude to find the next flash. "Sam," he said, "come here and take the wheel. Easy, now. Turn left to go left, right to go right, push forward to go down, pull back to go up, but make all the corrections with a very light touch. Leave the levers and shaft to me; I'll show you how to use them another day.

"See these two compasses, B and E? You see this arrow here, and this one here? Keep them pointed right where they are. If they drift off, and they will, make very slight corrections to ease the ship back on course. Here, let me show you."

Captain Pumpkin took the wheel. He hardly seemed to touch it, and the ship eased back to the correct course. He suggested to Sam, "Here, try again. It takes practice."

With Sam handling the wheel Captain Pumpkin took out a small mirror and a tiny pair of scissors and began carefully trimming his mustache. Sam couldn't help but be struck by the differences between his father and Captain Pumpkin. Sam's dad cared little about his appearance, usually wearing scuffed shoes and clothes that became rumpled almost the moment he put them on. Captain Pumpkin, Sam realized, was a bit vain, with his gleaming outfit and meticulous grooming.

As he worked at keeping the *Daisy* on course, Sam asked, "Why do you have a sailing ship? Why don't you use an engine?"

Captain Pumpkin laughed and explained, "There's no need. There is a wind that blows between the worlds, and within them, too. You can't see that wind or feel it, and I imagine your scientists haven't found it yet, but it's there. These sails are mostly just ordinary canvas, but they have threads of evitium woven in so they can catch both ordinary wind and the wind between the worlds. The keel of the ship is made of a serfidium/mangite alloy, serfidium being too soft and much too expensive to use alone. The keel is designed to be attracted to the Earth, which gives the wind something to push against. With the proper navigation, this ship can take us anywhere we want to go."

Sam glanced up for a moment. He noticed a storm cloud in the blue skies above them and heard a rustling flapping sound coming from above.

Captain Pumpkin looked up, too, and in terror seemed to say to himself, "Oh no!"

The flapping sound increased to a roar. Giant wings made of white paper covered with dense black writing created a wind that caused the *Daisy* to roll dangerously to starboard.

Mr. Bland descended from the sky. As he landed on the bow an unnatural calm enveloped the *Daisy*, and the wind that had powered the ship stopped blowing. The ship righted herself and stopped dead about three thousand feet in the air. A deathly silence descended upon the ship and crew.

Mr. Bland's wings folded themselves neatly into the back of his suit jacket. He adjusted his glasses, gray suit jacket, and dark blue tie, and glanced at his watch.

Sam had expected Mr. Bland to be a huge monster who looked obviously evil, like the bad guys in cartoons, but once Mr. Bland's wings were hidden in his suit jacket, he appeared pudgy, bald, and quite ordinary. To Sam, Mr. Bland did not look evil, he looked dull.

In a quiet voice that everyone strained to hear, Mr. Bland said, "The contract does not allow this." Taking a pen from his shirt pocket, he waved it slightly. Instantly, Captain Pumpkin began to split into Captain Kin and Captain Pump, and the masts started to rise out of the ship's hull.

Sam gathered his courage. "Wait!" he shouted. Looking at Mr. Bland, Sam found it difficult to believe anything bad about him. Mr. Bland reminded Sam of men in his town, like the pharmacist or the postmaster, who were very nice.

Mr. Bland stopped the movement of his pen and smiled kindly at Sam. “Yes?” he inquired politely.

“Um, well, sir, you banished Captain Pumpkin for two hundred years, and hasn’t it been more than that, sir?”

Mr. Bland smiled at Sam and replied, “Why, yes, you’re right. That is very smart of you.”

Sam felt a warm glow of pleasure at being praised by a grown-up.

“What is your name, young man?”

“Sam, sir.”

Mr. Bland reached out and they shook hands. “Pleased to meet you, Sam. My name is Mr. Bland.”

Sam expected Mr. Bland’s hand to be hard and strong, like his dad’s, but it felt soft, weak, and clammy. To Sam, he seemed less and less like a villain.

Mr. Bland explained in a warm, friendly, but very quiet way, “Sam, you know that Captain Pumpkin did very bad things. He was a pirate who robbed people. If he leaves Thunder Mountain, he will go back to his evil ways, and many innocent people will be hurt. You wouldn’t want that to happen, would you?”

Sam found himself agreeing with Mr. Bland, but then he thought about how admirable Captain Pumpkin now seemed. Randolph stood next to Sam and whispered, “Who do you want to grow up to be, Bland or Pumpkin?”

Sam thought for a moment, and then replied to Mr. Bland, “Captain Pumpkin promised he would give up piracy. Besides, I'm sure Captain Pumpkin has learned his lesson and will never go back to robbing people."

Mr. Bland patted Sam on the shoulder and smiled. "You are a true and loyal friend, and that is an admirable quality. But you have fallen in with a bad crowd. The ones you call your friends are very low creatures unworthy of your trust and friendship. A smart lad like you could do very well in life if he had the right training . . ." Mr. Bland gave Randolph, Bobbie Bear, and Captain Pumpkin a disdainful sneer and added, "and the right friends."

Randolph Coyote the Third stood next to Sam, his whole body alert. He whispered, "He's playing with your mind. Don't listen to him."

Mr. Bland's mask slipped slightly as he looked at Randolph Coyote the Third with barely concealed fury, but he recovered quickly. Mr. Bland smiled at Sam and continued in his quiet, emotionless voice, "Leave these creatures and come with me. I promise that if you are smart, loyal, and hardworking, you will have great wealth and power. I know it is possible because I used to be a lad just like you. Besides, who are you going to listen to, someone like me, who made a success of himself," Mr. Bland curled his lip, "Or a dog?"

Randolph whispered again, "Sam, he's full of beans. He says that piracy is bad, but he and Captain Pumpkin were in the piracy business together. Mr. Bland financed Pumpkin's pirate ship, led him to his victims, and took a ten percent cut. I'll bet he's still in the piracy business."

Mr. Bland's face contorted with rage. "Shut up, dog!" he hissed. Aiming his pen at Randolph, he gave it a quick snap. Randolph shrieked with pain and collapsed on the deck.

Without thinking, Sam kicked Mr. Bland in the shins and screamed, "Don't do that to my friend! It's been more than two hundred years. Captain Pumpkin is free to go. A deal's a deal!"

Mr. Bland forced himself to remain calm. "Pumpkin robbed one of my ships!" As he spoke, Mr. Bland's giant paper wings, with their dense lines of writing, unfurled.

It seemed to Sam that Mr. Bland then became even more boring on purpose, using boredom as a weapon. He spoke in a monotone so tiresome to Sam and his friends that they could hardly think clearly or move a muscle. Mr. Bland droned as though casting a spell, "The contract clearly states in Section 55, Subsection 34, Paragraph 56 that before joining back together again and vacating said premises, the party of the second part must give the party of the first part thirty days' notice by a notarized, courier delivered form meeting all the specifications set forth in Section 97, Subsection 109, Paragraph 567, and Addendum 768, Paragraph 438. If this is not done, and he joins together and vacates said premises, the curse remains in place for an additional two hundred years, Section 38, Subsection 82 notwithstanding."

As Mr. Bland mentioned parts of the contract, those parts lifted off his wings and buzzed around Captain Pumpkin's face like angry hornets. Captain Pumpkin stood on the deck stupefied with boredom. He tried to swat them away, but there were too many of them He began to move very slowly.

Mr. Bland gave a final loud flap of his wings, and Captain Pumpkin and the ship snapped apart, becoming Captain Pump with the hull and Captain Kin with the sails. All the sections of the contract flew back to Mr. Bland and settled on his wings.

Sam shook his head in an effort to clear the fogginess he felt seeping into every pore of his body. He looked at Mr. Bland in amazement, wondering how he ever could have thought of him as a decent, ordinary man.

Sam forced his weary mouth to form words. "You can't do that! It isn't fair!" he protested.

Mr. Bland adjusted his glasses and tie, glanced at his watch, looked at Sam and declared with quiet menace, "You are proving tiresome, and I must move on to my next appointment. You have a choice—swear total loyalty to me forever, or I will turn you into a bug and crush you under my shoe. You must give me your answer now."

Sam stood his ground and declared, "No!"

Mr. Bland raised his pen, prepared to strike, when Bobbie Bear stepped forward. She began rattling off sections of the contract that were in disagreement, canceling each other out. "Section 97, Subsection 109, Paragraph 567 is contradicted by Section 85, Subsection 34, Paragraph 28; Addendum 768, Paragraph 438 is contradicted by Section 25, Subsection 523, Paragraph 6 . . ."

Randolph Coyote the Third, recovered from both the pain and deadly boredom, staggered to his feet. He put on his best dog-about-to-attack pose, growled, and joined in. "Section 52, Subsection 9, Paragraph 78 is contradicted by Section 23, Subsection 15 . ."

As Bobbie Bear and Randolph spouted the conflicting sections, those parts of the contract lifted off Mr. Bland's wings, fought with each other, and attacked Mr. Bland.

While Mr. Bland swatted the sections away from his face, Captain Kin leaped from his sails down to the deck. He grabbed a boat hook and rushed at Mr. Bland screaming, "You pencil pushing peasant!"

Mr. Bland pulled a handkerchief out of his suit pocket and snapped it in Captain Kin's direction. Captain Kin's feet flew out from under him. He landed on the deck with a bone-jarring thud.

It quickly became obvious that Bobbie Bear knew the contract best, especially where the contradictions were. To stop her Mr. Bland snapped the handkerchief at her, causing her to drop on her back. Randolph picked her up and, using his snout, tossed her in the air. Mr. Bland continued snapping his handkerchief at her, but she flew with such skill that he kept missing. She would bounce off Randolph's snout and shoulders while reciting more and more conflicting sections.

Mr. Bland waved his pen back and forth furiously. The contradictory sections returned to his wings as fast as Bobbie Bear and Randolph could get them to take off.

Captain Kin rushed at Mr. Bland again, yelling at him, "Out of my way, you gutter-dwelling toad! I have worlds to conquer!"

Mr. Bland used his handkerchief to make Captain Kin drop on his back so hard Kin's mustache collapsed and he could hardly breathe.

At the top of a particularly high bounce, Bobbie Bear yelled out, "Captain Pump, we need your help!"

Captain Pump started to rush toward the fray, but he hesitated. He ran his hand through his unruly hair and thought, I did so many hateful things when I was a pirate. Maybe I deserve to be exiled to Thunder Mountain for another two hundred years. I need more time to think. He sat down on the deck looking confused.

Realizing the fight was dead even, Sam became terrified they might lose. Despite fearing Mr. Bland, Sam knew he could stand up to him. He yelled, "Section 13, Paragraph 2 contradicts Section 13, Paragraph 1!" while kicking Mr. Bland in his shins. Sam's effort tipped the balance.

As the three friends continued to yell out conflicting

sections, legalese lifted off Mr. Bland's wings and attacked him faster than he could get the writing to go back.

"It's not too late, Sam!" Mr. Bland yelled through the swarm. "Join me against this riffraff and I promise you great wealth and power!"

Sam answered by picking up the boat hook and swinging it at Mr. Bland, even though Sam couldn't aim the long pole very well.

Randolph continued calling out conflicting sections as he raised his leg and peed on Mr. Bland's pant leg.

Mr. Bland looked down at his leg. "Ahhh!" he yelled and jumped out of Randolph's way just as Sam swung the boat hook around. The boat hook swatted Mr. Bland's wings, and scattering more legalese into the air around his head.

A thunderous BANG shook the ship, causing everyone to jump with surprise as the masts dropped back into their steps with a rattling boom. Bobbie Bear landed on Randolph's shoulders and, looking around, was startled to see that Captain Pumpkin had pulled himself, and the *Daisy*, back together.

The captain stepped forward and asked Mr. Bland in a gentle voice, "Why are you doing this?"

Mr. Bland continued to swat legalese from his face, but his eyes shifted like those of a small child caught in a lie. He whined, "You robbed one of my ships!"

"Yes, I did, and I have paid a terrible price for it. But

our accounts are settled. My dreadful mistake happened over two hundred years ago. Why are you doing this now?"

Sam noticed Mr. Bland becoming a little smaller. "No one crosses me and gets away with it," he said, growing even smaller.

"What do you hope to gain by causing all this trouble? Sending me back to Thunder Mountain would be a very small-minded thing to do," Captain Pumpkin said gently.

Mr. Bland's suit, tie, and shoes were also made of legalese. So much of his clothes had turned back into contract clauses that his pants and shoes were rapidly vanishing and his tie attacked him, striking like a snake.

Mr. Bland, now about the size of Bobbie Bear and wearing shorts and half a suit jacket, threw a tantrum. He jumped up and down, stamped his feet, and yelled in a tiny, high pitched voice, "You robbed one of my ships! You robbed one of my ships!" Mr. Bland continued to shrink, but the tormenting contradictory contract sections did not. They swarmed all over him.

Mr. Bland looked ashamed of himself. Wearing nothing but his shirt and underwear, and reduced to the size of a moth, he leaped overboard with a sharp "EEEEEE!" He plunged straight down to shake off the swarming legalese, but to no avail.

Everyone on board the *Daisy* sat down for a moment to catch their breath. They looked at one another and smiled. Then the smiles turned to laughter, and the laughter turned to cheers. Randolph Coyote the Third let out a joyful victory howl. Sam felt very proud to be part of the group that had defeated Mr. Bland, the most powerful sorcerer in all the known worlds.

The wind that blows between the worlds filled the *Daisy*'s sails. Captain Pumpkin pulled the shaft up and pushed both levers forward. He adjusted the wheel as the ship moved up and ahead. With the ship back on course he sang:

> Yo ho ho and a flagon of tea.
> Bland almost got the better of me.
> But all of us made Mr. Bland go
> "EEEEEE!"
> Yo ho ho ho ho!

Chapter 19. Home

Bobbie Bear steered the *Daisy*, Captain Pumpkin whistled a happy tune while he polished his boots to a high shine, and Sam and Randolph sat on the deck leaning against a bulkhead talking. They watched through their goggles as Sam's home world in the Rainbow Flash got closer and closer until Bobbie Bear called out in a very loud voice, "White pollen away!"

"Why did she yell that so loudly?" Sam asked.

"When you hear that you are supposed to stop what you are doing and sit down. It's for safety. It's a warning that, in a few moments, we'll be blind, and if there's turbulence you don't want folks falling. But we are already sitting, so," Randolph said while stretching, "We don't have to do a thing, which is my favorite thing to do."

Sam and Randolph Coyote the Third continued chatting as they went through the Flash and into Sam's world.

Sam smiled as he thought back on the terror he had felt just before his first trip through a Flash. He realized with a shock that it had taken place only a few hours ago. Sam thought back, amazed, at how much had happened since he had left his bedroom.

When they got close to his house, at Captain Pumpkin's urging, Sam took control of the ship and soared and swooped over the still sleeping neighborhood. Sam couldn't remember ever being happier.

Captain Pumpkin stood next to Sam, gave the wheel slight corrections now and then to keep them all safe, and asked, "So, young Sam, any ideas of what you want to be when you grow up?"

"Well, I used to want to be a storyteller, but now I want to be a ship's captain and sail through flashes to other worlds. That is the most wonderful thing I can imagine."

Bobbie Bear, Randolph, and Captain Pumpkin all smiled. Bobbie Bear agreed, "Yes, very wonderful indeed."

"Please, can I stay with you?" Sam begged Captain Pumpkin. "I want to sail the *Daisy* forever!"

Captain Pumpkin put a comforting hand on Sam's shoulder. "Not yet, lad. You have a great deal to learn in school and much growing up to do. The world you live in may not be the only one, but the skills you need to function in it are the same ones you need to function in all the other worlds."

Reluctantly Sam brought the ship to a stop about a hundred feet above his house. Captain Pumpkin put out a sky anchor and Sam and Bobbie Bear got on Randolph's back for the short trip to Sam's bedroom window. Just before they left the *Daisy* Captain Pumpkin handed Sam the model ship and reminded him, "Here, don't forget this."

The three friends flew the short distance from the *Daisy* to Sam's home. When they arrived, they stood at Sam's bedroom window and waved good-bye to Captain Pumpkin

The Captain smiled, waved back, and turned his ship so the bowsprit pointed to the stars. As he zoomed off into the early morning sky, the three at the window could just barely hear Captain Pumpkin's booming voice singing:

> Yo ho ho, we put Bland on the run.
> His own legal phrases made him undone.
> And Sam got the courage to play and have fun!
> Yo ho ho ho ho!

Sam held the model of the *Daisy* to his chest. With tears streaming down his cheeks, he choked out, "I don't want to see him go."

Randolph licked the tears from Sam's face and comforted him. "Don't worry. I'm sure you two will meet again."

"Do you really think so?" Sam asked.

"Yes, I do."

Sam wiped his face. He hid the model ship deep in his toy-filled closet, got into his pajamas, and slept for an hour before his mother came to wake him for school. After breakfast, as Sam put on his jacket to leave for school, his mother said, "Wait a minute. That jacket has a hole in the sleeve. How did this happen?"

"Oh, I was walking along a narrow ledge on a cliff during a thunderstorm while a pirate was firing cannon balls at me. One of the cannonballs hit the cliff near my arm and a rock fragment tore my sleeve."

Sam's mother thought, *Even by Sam's standards, this is too much.* She crossed her arms, mustered all the patience she could, and said in a controlled voice, "Take off the jacket and I will mend it. You can wear a sweater today."

Sam went to his room and put on a sweater. Seeing Bobbie Bear and Randolph sleeping soundly in his bed, he smiled at them. But a stab of fear struck him as he thought, *What if none of this really had happened? What if I imagined the whole thing?*

In a panic, Sam dug through his closet. He breathed a sigh of relief when he saw the handsome model ship. Looking at it closely, he noticed a piece of paper poking out of one of the hatches. He took it out and read:

Dear Sam,

I want to thank you and your friends for all

you've done for me. You were very brave to
stand up to Mr. Bland. When you've learned
enough math, it would be my privilege to
teach you to navigate between the worlds.
Stay in touch.
Capt. P.

Sam smiled, clutched the note to his chest, and danced around the room, giddy with joy.

That day at school Sam saw his teacher in a new way, as a nice but terribly overworked lady who only wanted Sam to learn. And to everyone's surprise, at show-and-tell Sam volunteered to talk. Without revealing anything about flashes or how they are used, he told a story based on a small part of his own experiences. He told not only what happened but what it felt like to be there. For the first time, Sam felt the thrill of holding an audience spellbound. At the end of his tale they stood and applauded and cheered for several minutes. His teacher asked to publish Sam's story in the school newspaper.

At recess Sam played kickball with the other boys. He realized they were exactly his size and didn't kick the ball any harder than he did. He also swung fearlessly on the swings, which he now knew were just swings. As he flew higher and higher Sam thought they were fun but just a pale imitation of flying a coyote through a flash to another world.

About the Author

"The Flash Travelers book series was born when I least expected it – as stories I told my ten-year-old son Sam while driving to and from school," explains author Andrew Connan.

"The Flash Travelers books are buddy stories, adventure tales and stories about how an ordinary kid confronts his fears. And more stories kept coming."

As a kid, Andrew was that ordinary boy who grew up to be a silicon-valley tech writer. Working for companies like Oracle and Cisco Systems, he mastered the discipline of writing every day. But it took parenthood for him to realize that what he truly loved was writing adventure books for kids and teens.

So, join Andrew as he transforms Sam and his buddies – and ordinary kids everywhere – into Flash Travelers with adventures galore.

Books by Andrew Connan

If you liked this book, there's more to read in the ***Flash Travelers Series.***

Beyond the Rainbow Flash
Book 1 in the Flash Travelers Series

Coming soon!
The Rats of Finance
Book 2 in the Flash Travelers Series

Coming in 2018
Into the Land of Nightmares
Book 3 in the Flash Travelers Series

Made in the USA
Columbia, SC
13 April 2018